Grammar Girl's™

101 Troublesome Words You'll Master in No Time

Also by Mignon Fogarty

Grammar Girl's ™

101 Troublesome Words You'll Master in No Time

MIGNON FOGARTY

ST. MARTIN'S GRIFFIN ⁂ NEW YORK

GRAMMAR GIRL'S 101 TROUBLESOME WORDS YOU'LL MASTER IN NO TIME. Copyright
© 2012 by Mignon Fogarty, Inc. All rights reserved. Printed in the United States
of America. For information, address St. Martin's Press, 175 Fifth Avenue, New
York, N.Y. 10010.

Grammar Girl and Quick and Dirty Tips are trademarks of Mignon Fogarty, Inc.

www.stmartins.com

Book design by Meryl Sussman Levavi
Illustrations by Arnie Ten

Library of Congress Cataloging-in-Publication Data

Fogarty, Mignon.
    Grammar Girl's 101 troublesome words you'll master in no time / Mignon
Fogarty.—1st ed.
        p. cm.
    ISBN 978-0-312-57347-8
    1. English language—Usage.   2. English language—Terms and
phrases.   3. English language—Errors of usage.   I. Title.   II. Title: 101
troublesome words you'll master in no time.   III. Title: One hundred and
one troublesome words you'll master in no time.
    PE1460.F577 2012
    428.2—dc23

                                                        2012004622

First Edition: July 2012

10 9 8 7 6 5 4 3 2 1

For my mom, who wouldn't have
wanted me to shy away from
something just because it was hard.

Introduction

English is always changing, and that leaves us with troublesome words and phrases that are only sort of wrong. Some people insist the old ways to use words are the only correct ways, and other people use words in newer ways without even realizing the words are controversial. Like it or not, one way English changes is through misunderstandings and mistakes that gain a hold in the minds of enough people.

In other instances, we really have no rules. Some words have two acceptable spellings or two acceptable past tense forms. Sometimes experts take more of a "this way is better, but that way isn't wrong" approach. It's frustrating for people who just want to know what to write in their papers or e-mail messages.

Finally, some words are so confusing that people wish the rules would change, but they haven't.

In this book, I tackle many of these infuriating words—most of which I haven't covered in other books because they seemed too tricky—and I make judgments about which ones you should use without guilt today, and which ones you should shun a little longer. You likely will not agree with every choice, but at least I've taken a stand. In confusing cases like the 101 that follow, I've found that most people appreciate someone else doing the research, measuring the options, and making a recommendation.

Addicting

✦ **What's the Trouble?** **Addicting** is sometimes used interchangeably with *addictive*.

Some technical or medical books use *addicting* where a typical writer would likely use *addictive: Parents are told these drugs are not addicting*. Nevertheless, *addictive* is the more common term for describing something people struggle to quit.

What Should You Do?

Stick with *addictive* when you are trying to say a noun such as drug, video game, food, or lover has an unhealthy, nearly unbreakable hold on you.

> JOE FOX: **Do you know what? We are going to seduce them. We're going to seduce them with our square footage, and our discounts, and our deep armchairs, and . . .**
>
> JOE FOX, KEVIN: **Our cappuccino.**
>
> JOE FOX: **That's right. They're going to hate us at the beginning, but . . .**
>
> JOE FOX, KEVIN: **But we'll get 'em in the end.**
>
> JOE FOX: **Do you know why?**
>
> KEVIN: **Why?**
>
> JOE FOX: **Because we're going to sell them cheap books and legal** addictive **stimulants. In the meantime, we'll just put up a big sign: "Coming soon: a FoxBooks**

Addicting

> **superstore and the end of civilization as you know it."**
>
> —Tom Hanks as Joe Fox and Dave Chappelle as Kevin in the movie *You've Got Mail*

Reserve *addicting* for something or someone actively causing addiction.

> **Should cocaine moms be prosecuted for** addicting **their babies?**
>
> —*Jet* Magazine (headline)

African American

✦ What's the Trouble? People wonder about the difference between **African American** and *black*.

Acceptable names for people of color have changed over time and are likely to change again in the future. Today, both *African American* and *black* are considered respectful by most people in the black community.

African American is capitalized, but *black* is usually lower-cased unless it's part of the name of an organization (e.g., Congressional Black Caucus).

The Associated Press recommends a hyphen in *African-American,* but *The Chicago Manual of Style* recommends leaving it out in all compound nationalities (*African American, Italian American, Chinese American,* and so on).

Finally, *African American* sounds a little more formal than *black,* which could play a factor in your word choice.

What Should You Do?

For Americans of African descent, use *African American* or *black.* If the person you are describing is from another country, use another appropriate term, such as *Caribbean American.*

> **Opening tomorrow in New York, the documentary film *White Wash* explores the history of** black **surfing in America, painting a contrast to the global sport that is dominated by white males.**
>
> —James Sullivan in *USA Today*

African American **men living in areas with low sunlight are up to 3.5 times more likely to**

African American

**have Vitamin D deficiency than Caucasian
men and should take high levels of Vitamin D
supplements.**

—Northwestern University press release

For Americans of
African descent,
use African American
or black. If the
person you are
describing is from
another country, use
another appropriate
term, such as
Caribbean American.

Aggravate

✦ **What's the Trouble?** Some experts recommend avoiding **aggravate** when you mean "annoy" or "irritate," but such use is common and has a long history.

Aggravate came to English from a Latin word that means "to make heavier," and the argument that *aggravate* must mean "to make worse" instead of simply "annoy" or "irritate" hinges on that origin. In Latin, it meant to make things heavier, not just heavy—in other words, worse. However, people started using *aggravate* to mean "annoy" or "irritate" almost right away.

The adjective *aggravating* even more forcefully took on the meaning of "annoying" or "irritating." In fact, you'll find *aggravating* used in this way more than any other.

> **Ignorant people think it's the noise which fighting cats make that is so** aggravating, **but it ain't so; it is the sickening grammar that they use.**
>
> —Mark Twain in *A Tramp Abroad*

What Should You Do?

In formal situations or if you're feeling especially sticklerish, avoid using *aggravate* to mean "irritate."

> **I know you have an innate talent for rubbing people the wrong way, Jack, but why for the love of God would you** aggravate **the vice president?** [*Irritate* would be a better choice unless the vice president was already upset.]
>
> —Sasha Roiz as Parker in the movie *The Day After Tomorrow*

Aggravate

Using *aggravating* to mean "irritating" is less risky than using *aggravate* to mean "irritate," but some people may still object.

QUICK AND DIRTY TIP

When you hear cops on your favorite crime show talk about aggravated assault, remind yourself that *aggravated assault* is an assault that's <u>worse</u> than normal, just like an *aggravating comment* makes somebody's mood or situation <u>worse</u> than it already is.

Alright

✦ **What's the Trouble?** Nearly all usage guides condemn **alright**, but it occasionally shows up in the work of respected writers, and many people who aren't language experts think it's fine, or even the preferred spelling.

The *Oxford English Dictionary* calls *alright* a "frequent spelling of *all right*"—not quite saying outright that it is wrong, but making the implication. *The Columbia Guide to Standard American English* is clearer: "*All right* is the only spelling Standard English recognizes."

The word's history is little help. According to *Merriam-Webster's Dictionary of English Usage*, very early spellings included both one-word and two-word forms such as *ealriht* and *al rizt*.

Alright

With the pressure to save space in status updates and text messages, *alright* is likely to gain currency rather than fade. The "saves space" argument is not new; an early proponent of *alright* over *all right* mentioned the cost savings of sending cable messages using *alright*.

Until popular usage guides such as *The Chicago Manual of Style* and *AP Stylebook* give their stamp of approval to *alright*, the word will be edited out of most professional work. However, one telling sign is that it's easy to find quotations on GoodReads.com, transcribed by people who are likely to be above-average readers, that substitute *alright* when *all right* appears in the original book. I predict *alright* will eventually win.

What Should You Do?

Stick with *all right* unless you wish to be part of the charge to legitimize *alright*, which right now is a fringe position.

> **Is Bill** alright? . . . **Cowley thinks I'm a Simple Simon. I'm a fool** alright.
>
> —Jack Kerouac in a personal letter to Allen Ginsberg, Peter Orlovsky, William S. Burroughs, and Alan Ansen

Alternate

✦ What's the Trouble? Traditionalists have sometimes made a distinction between the adjectives **alternate** and *alternative*.

Although some style guides try to make a distinction between *alternate* and *alternative*, most concede that both adjectives are acceptable when you mean "substitute": *Find an alternate route. Find an alternative route.*

When people or events are taking turns, however, the only correct choice is *alternate*: *Mr. Brown has his son on alternate Saturdays. Alternate* is also the only correct choice when you're using the word as a noun: *He was an alternate on the jury.*

What Should You Do?

Don't fret about the adjectives *alternate* and *alternative*. Either is acceptable when you mean "substitute" and most other uses are obvious to native English speakers.

> **BURTON "GUS" GUSTER: How should we introduce ourselves? Don't say "psychic." They'll shut you off. Pick something vague, like** Alternative **Tactics Division.**
>
> **SHAWN SPENCER: How about the Bureau of Magic and Spell Casting?**
>
> —Dulé Hill as Gus and James Roday as Shawn in the TV series *Psych*

Bureau of Magic and Spell Casting

Alternate

PENNY: What is he doing?

LEONARD HOFSTADTER: It's a little hard to explain. He's pretending to be in an alternate **universe where he occupies the same physical space as us, but cannot perceive us.**

SHELDON COOPER: Oh, don't flatter yourself. I'm just ignoring you.

—Kaley Cuoco as Penny, John Galecki as Leonard, and Jim Parsons as Sheldon in the TV series *The Big Bang Theory*

Alternative

✦ **What's the Trouble?** A few people say that **alternative** can only be used when there are two choices.

The Latin root of *alternative* is *alter*, which means "the other of two" or simply "the other." Based on this etymology, some usage writers in the 1800s began suggesting that *alternative* should be used only when describing a choice between two options—not three or more. However, few modern sources support the notion, and *Merriam-Webster's Dictionary of English Usage* reports that some have gone as far as to call it a fetish or pedantry.

What Should You Do?

Feel free to use *alternative* for three or more choices unless you have reason to believe you're writing for someone who hangs on to the outdated rule.

> [L]ibraries should be open to all—except the censor. We must know all the facts and hear all the alternatives and listen to all the criticisms. Let us welcome controversial books and controversial authors. For the Bill of Rights is the guardian of our security as well as our liberty.
>
> —John F. Kennedy in the *Saturday Review*

American

✦ **What's the Trouble?** **American** is the only single word we have to refer to "a citizen of the United States of America" (*USican?*), but technically, an *American* is "anyone who lives in North America, Central America, or South America."

We, the people, have been calling ourselves Americans since before our country was even founded (as have our detractors). Although all people of the American continents are actually Americans, most readers in the United States and Europe assume that an *American* is a U.S. citizen since that is how the word is most commonly used.

What Should You Do?

Despite its failings, use *American* to refer to "a citizen of the United States of America." No better term exists. Feel free to feel guilty.

> **The Constitution only guarantees the** American **people the right to pursue happiness. You have to catch it yourself.**
>
> —Benjamin Franklin

Ax

✦ **What's the Trouble?** The handheld tool for chopping wood has two spellings: **ax** and *axe*.

The standard American spelling is *ax*, and the standard British spelling is *axe*. Axe body spray, which is heavily advertised in the United States, was created by a British company and first launched in France.

If you'd like to feel superior to the British, the *Oxford English Dictionary* says that the *ax* spelling is better than *axe* in terms of "etymology, phonology, and analogy."

What Should You Do?

In America, spell the word *ax*.

> **In this country people don't respect the morning. An alarm clock violently wakes them up, shatters their sleep like the blow of an ax, and they immediately surrender themselves to deadly haste. Can you tell me what kind of day can follow a beginning of such violence?**
>
> —Milan Kundera in *Farewell Waltz*

Back

✦ What's the Trouble? Back is often redundant when used in phrases such as *refer back*.

Since the prefix *re-* means "back" in words such as *retreat, revert, reply,* and *respond,* to add *back* after these words is usually redundant. (*Re-* can mean "again" in other words, such as *repeat.*)

In some cases, however, *back* can subtly change the meaning of the sentence. For example, in the *Gatsby* quotation below, *retreat back* gives a sense of two monsters briefly coming out of a hiding place and then going back to the same place.

What Should You Do?

If you can drop *back* from phrases such as *refer back* without changing the meaning of your sentence, do it.

> **They were careless people, Tom and Daisy—
> they smashed up things and creatures and
> then retreated** back **into their money or their
> vast carelessness, or whatever it was that
> kept them together, and let other people clean
> up the mess they had made.**
>
> —F. Scott Fitzgerald in *The Great Gatsby*

Begs the Question

✦ **What's the Trouble?** It's rare to see **begs the question** used the right way.

Begs the question comes from formal logic, in which the person making an argument does so in a way that simply states that the premise is true instead of proving it is true. It can be a premise that's independent from the conclusion or, in a simpler form, the conclusion can be a circular restatement of the premise.

It does not mean "raises the question" or "begs that I ask the question."

For example, let's say Squiggly is trying to convince Aardvark that chocolate is health food. Squiggly would be *begging the question* if he argued that chocolate is healthy because it's good for you. He hasn't proven that chocolate is healthy; he's simply used a synonym for *healthy* as his argument. He's *begged* the listener to accept the question (is chocolate healthy?) as the conclusion (chocolate is healthy). When debaters *beg the question*, they base their arguments on a faulty premise.

Here's an example of the common, wrong, way to use *begs the question*:

> **Being president of this country is entirely about character. For the record: yes, I am a card-carrying member of the ACLU. But the more important question is why aren't you, Bob? Now, this is an organization whose sole purpose is to defend the Bill of Rights, so it naturally** begs the question: **Why would a**

senator, his party's most powerful spokesman and a candidate for president, choose to reject upholding the Constitution?

—Michael Douglas as President Andrew Shepherd
in the movie *The American President*

What Should You Do?

Reestablishing the traditional meaning of *begs the question* is a lost cause, but even though almost nobody will realize you've made an error, there's also no reason to misappropriate the phrase. If you mean "raises the question" or "begs that I ask the question," say *raises the question* or *begs that I ask the question*.

Bemused

+ **What's the Trouble? Bemused** can be confused with *amused*.

Bemused means "confused, bewildered, or baffled," and has nothing to do with amusement or humor. The eighteenth-century poet Alexander Pope first used the word to describe someone who was muddled by liquor or had found a muse in beer.

What Should You Do?

Think of *bemused* as similar to *befuddled* and use it only to describe someone who is confused. Avoid using *bemused* in situations where the context is ambiguous enough to leave the reader wondering whether you mean "amused" or "confused."

> **Draco was on the upper landing, pleading with another masked Death Eater.**
>
> **Harry stunned the Death Eater as they passed: Malfoy looked around, beaming, for his savior, and Ron punched him from under the cloak. Malfoy fell backward on top of the Death Eater, his mouth bleeding, utterly bemused.**
>
> **"And that's the second time we've saved your life tonight, you two-faced bastard!" Ron yelled.**
>
> —J. K. Rowling in the novel *Harry Potter and the Deathly Hallows*

Between

✦ What's the Trouble? Some people
believe **between** should only refer to two things.

Popular usage guides and schoolbooks have stated that *between* can only be used when you refer to two things, and that *among* should be your choice when there are more.

> **See, the only difference** between **a winner and a loser is character. Every man has a price to charge, and a price to pay.**
>
> —Taylor Kitsch as Remy LeBeau in the movie
> *X-Men Origins: Wolverine*

Although *between* does work for sentences involving two choices, the "rule" is an oversimplification and does not accurately represent broader common and historical uses of *between*.

What Should You Do?

Between has always been used to indicate a choice or relationship between many different individual items or people. Native English speakers naturally make this choice (note how wrong *among* would sound in the examples below), and modern usage guides support this use of *between*.

> Between **Monica, Phoebe, Chandler and Ross—if you had to—who would you punch?**
>
> —Matt LeBlanc as Joey Tribbiani in the TV series *Friends*

> **I had a hard time choosing the right adjectives. I couldn't decide** between **childish, juvenile, and just plain old annoying.**
>
> —Valarie Ray Miller as Agent Bryn Fillmore
> in the TV series *NCIS*

Billion

✦ **What's the Trouble?** At times, **billion** has meant a different amount in American English than it has in other English-speaking countries.

Believe it or not, the world has two naming systems for large power-of-ten numbers such as a billion and a trillion: the short scale and the long scale. In the long scale, a billion is 1,000,000,000,000 (10^{12}) and in the short scale, a billion is 1,000,000,000 (10^9). Britain traditionally used the long scale, but Americans adopted the short scale. What a mess!

Fortunately, Britain and many other countries switched to the "short scale" in the mid-1970s, and *billion* usually now means the same amount in all English-speaking countries (France, Germany, Italy, Spain, Denmark, Finland, and other European countries currently use the long scale.)

What Should You Do?

Today, you can safely use *billion* to mean 1,000,000,000. When you are reading old or translated documents, however, be aware of their country of origin and remember that the meaning of *billion* could be 1,000,000,000,000. *Billions,* plural, is also often used metaphorically to describe an unfathomable amount.

> **I know this will come as a shock to you, Mr. Goldwyn, but in all history, which has held** billions **and** billions **of human beings, not a single one ever had a happy ending.**
>
> —A conversation between Dorothy Parker and Sam Goldwyn related in *Dorothy Parker: What Fresh Hell Is This?* by Marion Meade

Biweekly

✦ What's the Trouble? Biweekly means two contradictory things.

The prefix *bi-* can mean "two" or "twice." Think of a bicycle with two wheels or bifocals with two lenses. Unfortunately, when the *bi-* prefix is added to *weekly*, it can mean every two weeks or twice a week.

It's not just a problem of people being confused or misunderstanding the meaning. Dictionary definitions for *biweekly* actually include both meanings: "every two weeks" and "twice a week."

What Should You Do?

Although it's always sad to abandon words, the safest choice is to avoid *biweekly* and *bimonthly* and instead just use *twice a week* or *every other week*.

> **I was nothing if not determined; at least** twice a week **I would wear bright, pretty clothes. I was afraid if I didn't, I'd forget who I was. I'd turn into what I felt like: a grungy, weapon-bearing, pissy, resentful vengeance-hungry bitch.**
>
> —Karen Marie Moning in *Faefever*

> **Yeah, like high school. It's easy to date there. I mean, we all had so much in common. Being monster food** every other week, **for instance.**
>
> —Charisma Carpenter as Cordelia in the TV series *Angel*

Bring and Take

✦ **What's the Trouble?** The standard rule doesn't always lead you to an answer.

In many cases the choice between **bring** and **take** is easy: People bring things to your current location, and take things away from your current location. *Bring me cotton candy. Take away this broccoli.* It's all focused on a place.

The rules fall apart, however, when you consider the future or a location where nobody has arrived yet. Do you bring rum cake to the school bazaar or do you take rum cake to the school bazaar? It simply depends on where you want to place the emphasis of the sentence—which perspective you want to adopt.

If you want to focus on the school and write from the perspective of the bazaar, you bring the cake to the bazaar. If you want to focus on your kitchen and write from the perspective of home, then you take the cake to the bazaar (which puts the focus on taking it away from your home).

What Should You Do?

When you start writing about the future and have to choose between *bring* and *take,* imagine where you are in the scenario, and make your word choice based on that location.

Bring and Take

DEXTER MORGAN: Hey guys, I need your addresses for the wedding and I need to know if you're bringing **dates.**

ANGEL BATISTA: Can we bring **just friends?**

VINCE MASUKA: I never bring **dates to a wedding. Best man always hooks up with the maid of honor.**

DEXTER MORGAN: The maid of honor is Rita's daughter. She's ten.

[Note how they could have used *take*, but also how it would have subtly changed the focus of the sentence. *Bring* causes you to imagine them at the wedding, whereas *take* would cause you to imagine them at home getting ready or picking up their dates.]

—Michael C. Hall as Dexter, David Zayas as Angel, and C. S. Lee as Vince in the TV series *Dexter*

Cactus

✦ **What's the Trouble? Cactus** has two acceptable plural
forms: *cactuses* and *cacti*.

Cactus comes from the Greek word *kaktos,* which made its
way into Latin (where the plural became *cacti*) and then
through Latin into English.

Foreign words that become established in English often lose
their foreign plural form in favor of a Standard English plural
that ends in *s.* Yet, the foreign form can continue to coexist
with the new English plural or can survive in isolated contexts
as is the case with *cactus.* Although *cactuses* is common in
general writing, *cacti* is still dominant in botanical writing.

What Should You Do?

If you write for gardening magazines, nurseries, or botanical
audiences use *cacti.* Otherwise, use *cactuses.*

> **Those who have never visited the American
> Southwest tend to have some misconceptions.
> The most common one is that the whole place
> is a hot desert studded with saguaro** cactuses.
>
> —Lesley S. King, Don Laine, Karl Samson in
> *Frommer's American Southwest*

> **The propagation of** cacti **from seeds is one of
> those things which require an immense
> amount of patience. Most of these plants are
> naturally slow growers and the time needful
> to produce a flowering-size plant from seed
> would in many species be as much as the
> span of a man's life.**
>
> —S. Leonard Bastin in *Scientific American*

Celtic

✦ **What's the Trouble?** People who speak languages in the family that includes Breton, Welsh, Irish, Scotch Gaelic, and Cornish can be called **Celtic** or Keltic.

Although *Celtic* is the more common spelling in America, you'll also see *Keltic,* and dictionaries say both are acceptable.

The argument for *Keltic* is that it originally comes from the Greek word *keltoi*, but although the people the Greeks called the Keltoi may have spoken an early form of Celtic, they didn't inhabit the British Isles—the lands we think of as Celtic. Instead, they lived in a large region of Western Europe called Gaul.

On the other hand, the argument for *Celtic* is that the word came into English not directly from Greek, but through French, and the French word is *celtique*.

It's even confusing in Scotland. Glasgow has a soccer team called the Celtic Football Club, even though most people living in Scotland would refer to themselves as Keltic.

What Should You Do?

The *Keltic* spelling and hard-*k* pronunciation are greatly preferred by people who study the culture and language, to the point that if you call it anything other than Keltic, they're likely to look down on you. But in general writing, *Celtic* prevails, and if you are attending a basketball game in Boston or a football game in Glasgow, you're rooting for the Celtics.

> **After the conquest, with the spread of Roman civilisation, Late** Keltic **art rapidly disappeared in the south of Britain, hitherto its chief centre;**

nevertheless, it persisted in Scotland and
Ireland till the coming of Christianity, where
and when it was used by the early Christians
to decorate their monuments and metalwork,
and to embellish their illuminated manu-
scripts.

—Norman Ault in *Life in Ancient Britain*

We Irish prefer embroideries to plain cloth.
To us Irish, memory is a canvas—stretched,
primed, and ready for painting on. We love
the "story" part of the word "history," and
we love it trimmed out with color and drama,
ribbons and bows. Listen to our tunes,
observe a Celtic scroll: we always decorate
our essence.

—Frank Delaney in *Tipperary: A Novel*

Companies

✦ **What's the Trouble?** People wonder whether to refer to a company as *who* or *that*.

Companies are entities, but they are run by people. An argument could be made for using either *who* or *that* as the pronoun when you're writing about a company that takes an action, particularly since U.S. courts have ruled that companies are people in most legal senses. However, the preferred style is to refer to a company as an entity and use the pronouns *it* and *that*: *We want to buy stock in a* <u>company that</u> *makes hot air balloons*.

If you want to highlight that people in the company are behind some action or decision, name them and use *who*: *Floating Baskets was driven to bankruptcy by its* <u>senior directors who</u> *took too many expensive Alaskan joy rides*.

What Should You Do?

Stick with the pronouns *it* and *that* when referring to *companies*.

> **The move brought an end to Mr. Icahn's two-month fight to squeeze more value out of a century-old** company that **is facing tough competition from generics but which investors generally see as well run.**
>
> —Paul Ziobro in *The Wall Street Journal*

Couldn't Care Less

✦ **What's the Trouble?** People say they *could care less* when, logically, they mean they **couldn't care less**.

The phrase *I couldn't care less* originated in Britain and made its way to the United States in the 1950s. The less logical phrase *I could care less* appeared in the United States about a decade later.

In the early 1990s, the well-known Harvard linguist Stephen Pinker argued that the way most people say *could care less*—the way they emphasize the words—implies they are being ironic or sarcastic. Other linguists have argued that the type of sound at the end of *couldn't* is naturally dropped by sloppy or slurring speakers.

Regardless of the reason people say they *could care less,* it is one of the more common language peeves because of its illogical nature. To say you *could care less* means you have a bit of caring left, which is not what the speakers seem to intend. The proper *couldn't care less* is still the dominant form in print, but *could care less* has been steadily gaining ground since its appearance in the 1960s.

What Should You Do?

Stick with *couldn't care less*.

> **JULIET O'HARA: Guess what today is.**
>
> **CARLTON LASSITER: It's not one of those touchy-feely holidays invented by card companies to goad me into buying a present for someone I** couldn't care less **about, is it?**
>
> —Maggie Lawson as O'Hara and Timothy Omundson as Lassiter in the TV series *Psych*

Data

+ **What's the Trouble?** **Data** is used as both a singular and plural noun.

Although *data* is a plural word in Latin, it's much more likely to be used as a singular noun in English. The *Oxford English Dictionary* includes both plural and singular definitions, although the editors note that in Latin, *datum* is singular and *data* is plural.

Although you are less likely to be criticized by sticklers for treating *data* as plural, phrases such as *the data are compelling* are less common than *the data is compelling* in news articles, and treating *data* as plural can sound odd to readers.

What Should You Do?

Garner's Modern American Usage calls *data* a skunked term, meaning you can't win—whether you treat it as singular or plural, you'll get in trouble. Try to write around the problem, for example, by using *data point* or *information*.

In general writing, if *information* won't work because you're using *data* as a mass noun to mean "information collected in a scientific way," *data* can be singular; however, in scientific writing, always treat *data* as plural.

> **Remember the cell phone that was never used? Well, it was used. Only all the** data **was hard-erased.** [*Information* would be a safer choice.]
>
> —Pauley Perrette as Abby Sciuto in the TV series *NCIS*

> **Few weather stations dot remote and high-altitude locales and where they do exist their** data **are often incomplete.**
>
> —Brian Handwerk in *National Geographic*

Decimate

✦ **What's the Trouble?** Some people cling to the belief that because of the prefix *deci-*, the word **decimate** can only mean "reduction by 10 percent."

The Roman military wasn't as interested in justice as it was in order. We get the word *decimate* from its practice of punishing mutinous units by having the men draw lots. Those drawing the unlucky 10 percent were killed by the remaining 90 percent of their comrades. *Decimate* has its etymological root in the Latin word for *tenth,* and shares that root with words like *decimal* and *decimeter.*

Because of these historical and etymological roots, some people believe that the only proper way to use *decimate* is to talk about something reduced by precisely 10 percent. Usage experts disagree. *Merriam-Webster's Dictionary of English Usage (MWDEU),* for example, notes that *decimate* has never been used this way in English. Although there is an entry for the "reduction by 10 percent" meaning in the *Oxford English Dictionary (OED),* it contains no example sentences, which is unusual. The *MWDEU* editors believe that the *OED* definition was included merely to bridge the gap between the Roman practice and the Standard English meaning, which is "a massive or severe reduction."

What Should You Do?

Use *decimate* without fear to describe a huge culling or loss. Because of its roots, *decimate* is particularly well used when describing significant casualties in a population of military troops but it can be used to describe any extreme loss. Beware of using it to describe a complete loss, however. That use is incorrect.

Decimate

Who, in the midst of passion, is vigilant against illness? Who listens to the reports of recently decimated **populations in Spain, India, Bora Bora, when new lips, tongues and poems fill the world?**

—Lauren Groff in *Delicate Edible Birds: And Other Stories*

Dialogue

✦ **What's the Trouble?** **Dialogue** has two acceptable spellings, and many people object to the word's newer use as a verb.

Although *dialog* is an acceptable spelling, *dialogue* is more common.

The real controversy is whether it's OK to use *dialogue* as a verb that means "to talk" or "to exchange ideas." The use has been around for centuries, but it seems to have become trendy in business circles in the last few decades. Although using *dialogue* this way isn't wrong, many sources criticize it as jargon or faddish.

What Should You Do?

Avoid *dialogue* as a verb unless it's common in your circles. It's not wrong, but can be viewed as annoying or pretentious.

> **Real life is sometimes boring, rarely conclusive and boy, does the** dialogue **need work.**
>
> —Sarah Rees Brennan, Irish writer

> **In coming months, Texas airports will continue** dialoguing **with each other to learn ways to best serve the public and the communities that depend on commercial air service.** [*Communicating* would be a better choice.]
>
> —Houston Airport System press release

Dilemma

✦ What's the Trouble? Some style guides say **dilemma** should be used only to describe a choice between two unpleasant options, but a broader meaning is pervasive.

The *di-* prefix in *dilemma* means "two" or "double," which lends support to the idea that *dilemma* should be used only to describe a choice between two alternatives. The Associated Press and *Garner's Modern American Usage* support that limitation, and go further, saying that *dilemma* should be used only for a choice between two unpleasant options.

Nevertheless, *Garner's* also concedes that other uses are "ubiquitous." *Merriam-Webster's Dictionary of English Usage* and the *Columbia Guide to Standard American English* say it's fine to use *dilemma* to describe any serious predicament, and *The American Heritage Guide to Contemporary Usage and Style* takes an intermediate position. What's a writer to do? (Is it a dilemma?)

What Should You Do?

Unless you're following a style guide that requires you to limit *dilemma* to a choice between two bad options, it's acceptable to use *dilemma* to describe a difficult problem, even when alternatives aren't involved, or to use *dilemma* to describe a difficult choice between pleasant options. Still, you'll seem most clever when you use *dilemma* to describe a choice between two bad options. In other instances, before using *dilemma,* ask yourself if another word, such as *problem,* would work better.

QUICK AND DIRTY TIP

To remember that *dilemma* is best used for a choice between two things, think of the idiom *on the horns of a dilemma* and picture the mascot of the University of Texas—a longhorn steer with two huge horns.

You see the dilemma, **don't you? If you don't kill me, precogs were wrong and precrime is over. If you do kill me, you go away, but it proves the system works. The precogs were right. So, what are you going to do now?** [Particularly nice use of *dilemma*.]

—Tom Cruise as John Anderton in the movie
Minority Report

There are two dilemmas **that rattle the human skull. How do you hold onto someone who won't stay? And how do you get rid of someone who won't go?** [*Problems, questions,* or *quandaries* would have been a better choice.]

—Danny DeVito as Gavin in the movie
The War of the Roses

Done

✦ **What's the Trouble?** Some people say you can't use **done** to mean "finished" unless you're talking about food.

Although *done* has been used to mean "finished" for centuries, admonitions against it started surfacing in the early 1900s. No reasoning was given in the first published style guide that made the declaration. *Merriam-Webster's Dictionary of English Usage* speculates the advice was based on bias against the usage's "Irish, Scots and U.S." origin.

The "rule" against *done* has been widely taught in schools, but no historical pattern, logic, or modern usage guide supports it.

What Should You Do?

Don't be afraid to use *done,* although *finished* and *through* are fine too.

I'm cookie dough. I'm not done baking. I'm not finished becoming whoever the hell it is I'm gonna turn out to be. I make it through this, and the next thing, and the next thing, and maybe one day, I turn around and realize I'm ready. I'm cookies.

—Sarah Michelle Gellar as Buffy in the TV series *Buffy the Vampire Slayer*

Donut

✦ What's the Trouble? Donut is a simplified variant of *doughnut*.

A *doughnut* is literally a nut (ball) of dough. According to the *Oxford English Dictionary,* the name was first reported by American author Washington Irving (using the pen name Diedrich Knickerbocker) in 1809. The sweet treat he was describing resembled what today we'd call doughnut holes rather than the puffy rings we now call *doughnuts*.

The *donut* spelling appeared about one hundred years later but did not immediately thrive. However, its use has grown steadily and significantly since Dunkin' Donuts was founded in 1950.

What Should You Do?

Stick with *doughnut* (unless, perhaps, you're writing ad copy for deep-fried sugary dough).

> **A paradox, the** doughnut **hole. Empty space, once, but now they've learned to market even that. A minus quantity; nothing, rendered edible. I wondered if they might be used— metaphorically, of course—to demonstrate the existence of God. Does naming a sphere of nothingness transmute it into being?**
>
> —Margaret Atwood in *The Blind Assassin*

Do's and Don'ts

✦ **What's the Trouble?** The spelling of **do's and don'ts** is inconsistent.

Generally, you don't use apostrophes to make words or abbreviations plural (e.g., *CDs, 1970s, hats*), but we have a few exceptions. For example, you can use apostrophes when they help eliminate confusion, which happens most often with single letters. *Mind your p's and q's* is the typical spelling, and we write that the word *aardvark* has 3 *a*'s, not 3 *a*s.

Do's and don'ts is an especially unusual exception. The apostrophe in the contraction *don't* seems to make people want to use an apostrophe to make *do* plural (*do's and don'ts*) but then to be consistent, you'd also have to use an apostrophe to make *don't* plural, which becomes downright ugly (*do's and don't's*).

Style guides and usage books don't agree. *The Chicago Manual of Style* and others recommend *dos and don'ts,* the Associated Press and others recommend *do's and don'ts,* and *Eats, Shoots & Leaves* recommends *do's and don't's.*

What Should You Do?

Unless your editor wishes otherwise, if you write books, spell it *dos and don'ts;* and if you write for newspapers, magazines, or the Web, spell it *do's and don'ts.* If you're writing for yourself, spell it any way you want.

> **Who better than a 16-year-old girl to help navigate the exhausting social networking world of love and the** do's and don'ts **of relationship statuses?**
>
> —Alison Bonaguro writing for CMT.com

Drag

✦ **What's the Trouble?** *Dragged* is the proper past tense of the verb **drag**, but *drug* is a common variant, especially in the South.

Drag is a regular verb, which means the past tense is *dragged*. English tends to like regular verbs, and irregular verbs tend to become regularized over time (for example, the past tense of *chide* used to be *chode*, but now it's *chided*). Yet an odd thing has happened with *drag* in America and especially in the South: people started using *drug* (the irregular form) instead of *dragged* (the regular form) for the past tense.

What Should You Do?

Although *drug* is clearly part of some dialects, it's not considered Standard English. Avoid it, especially in writing.

> **And as he drove on, the rain clouds** dragged **down the sky after him for, though he did not know it, Rob McKenna was a Rain God. All he knew was that his working days were miserable and he had a succession of lousy holidays. All the clouds knew was that they loved him and wanted to be near him, to cherish him and water him.**
>
> —Douglas Adams in *The Ultimate Hitchhiker's Guide to the Galaxy*

Earth

✦ What's the Trouble? **Earth** isn't treated like the names of other planets.

In English, the general rule is that we capitalize the formal names of things and places (e.g., *Golden Gate Bridge, San Francisco*), so we capitalize the names of other planets: *Jupiter, Mars,* and so on. For some unknown reason, however, we treat *earth* differently. Sometimes it's capitalized and sometimes it's lowercased, and there doesn't seem to be a hard-and-fast rule.

Typically, when *earth* is proceeded by *the,* it's lowercased; and typically, when *earth* is listed with the names of the other planets, it's capitalized—but you can find exceptions to even these patterns.

Of course, when we're just using *earth* as another word for *dirt,* it's always lowercase.

What Should You Do?

If you're a professional writer, check your publication's style guide to see what it recommends. If you're writing for yourself, check a style guide or decide on your own when you will capitalize *earth* and be consistent.

> **For instance, on the planet** Earth, **man had always assumed that he was more intelligent than dolphins because he had achieved so much—the wheel, New York, wars and so on—whilst all the dolphins had ever done was muck about in the water having a good time. But conversely, the dolphins had always**

**believed that they were far more intelligent
than man—for precisely the same reasons.**

—Douglas Adams in *The Hitchhiker's Guide to the Galaxy*

**It can hardly be a coincidence that no
language on** earth **has ever produced the
expression, "As pretty as an airport."**

—Douglas Adams in *The Long Dark Tea-Time of the Soul*

Eldest

✦ **What's the Trouble?** English has two sets of words you can use to talk about relative age.

The adjectives *elder* and *older* and **eldest** and *oldest* mean largely the same things. You can usually use them interchangeably when you're talking about people; however, you can't use *elder* and *eldest* to describe things. *Elder* and *eldest* also tend to sound more formal. *Elder* is also more common in set phrases that imply seniority such as *elder statesman*.

Do take care to use them in the right context though. *Elder* and *older* are comparatives, so you use them when you are comparing two people. If you have two daughters, you would talk about your elder or older daughter. *Eldest* and *oldest* are superlatives, so you use them when you're comparing more than two people. If you have three daughters, you would talk about your eldest or oldest daughter.

What Should You Do?

Use *elder* and *older* and *eldest* and *oldest* interchangeably when you're talking about people. Only use *older* and *oldest* when you're talking about things.

> **The** oldest **and strongest emotion of mankind is fear, and the** oldest **and strongest kind of fear is fear of the unknown.**
>
> [Note how only *oldest* works here.]
>
> —H. P. Lovecraft in "Supernatural Horror in Literature"

Ruin, eldest **daughter of Zeus, she blinds us all, that fatal madness—she with those delicate feet of hers, never touching the earth, gliding over the heads of men to trap us all. She entangles one man, now another.**

[Note how *oldest* or *eldest* would work.]

—Homer in *The Iliad*

Else's

✦ What's the Trouble? Spell checkers confuse people by erroneously marking **else's** incorrect.

In the early 1800s, the apostrophe went on the first part of *somebody else,* as in *somebody's else problem.* Usage shifted, however, and today the apostrophe goes on the second part. The only correct form today is *somebody else's, anybody else's, everyone else's,* and so on.

Unfortunately, electronic spell checkers can't seem to get this one right. They regularly mark *else's* as incorrect, causing some people to doubt whether the words they've heard their whole life are correct. Never rely entirely on spell checkers; they occasionally make big errors such as marking *else's* incorrect, and they can't tell when you've used a homonym instead of misspelled a word (e.g., *its* for *it's*). Think of your spell checker as something that merely highlights words you should double-check.

What Should You Do?

Ignore your spell checker when it marks *else's* incorrect.

> I've been making a list of the things they don't teach you at school. They don't teach you how to love somebody. They don't teach you how to be famous. They don't teach you how to be rich or how to be poor. They don't teach you how to walk away from someone you don't love any longer. They don't teach you how to know what's going on in someone else's mind. They don't teach you what to say to someone who's dying. They don't teach you anything worth knowing.
>
> —Neil Gaiman in *The Sandman, Vol. 9: The Kindly Ones*

E-mail Versus Email

✦ What's the Trouble? Some style guides recommend **e-mail** (with a hyphen) and other style guides recommend **email** (without a hyphen).

E-mail stands for "electronic mail," and it was originally hyphenated because it was usually a compound modifier in *electronic-mail message*. Today, although some people object to *email* alone, such use is widespread and standard: *I got twenty e-mails in the last hour.*

Email has been widely written without the hyphen for years, and in 2010, the Associated Press changed their recommended spelling from *e-mail* to *email*, saying they were bowing to common usage.

At the time this book was published, some newspapers were holding off on adopting AP style and were still using *e-mail*. *The Chicago Manual of Style* still recommends *e-mail*, even though the writer of *Chicago*'s Q&A section had indicated a fondness for *email*.

What Should You Do?

Whether you like it or not, fighting for *e-mail* is a lost cause. I prefer it. I still use it. But it will be a relic in ten to twenty years—like *per-cent*. If you're writing for a publication that uses a specific style guide, follow their style. If you're writing for yourself, it's generally safe to use whichever spelling you prefer.

> **In an email, [Mark] Malkoff said of his visit [to the Netherlands]: "Did you know they have urinals on the street? I had no clue. Some of the fun stuff I did included: asking Dutch citizens to donate money to help pay off the**

U.S. debt, go running in wooden clogs (turns out it hurts!), hang a drawing I did in the bathroom at the Van Gogh Museum, covering myself in birdseed in Dam Square while dozens of pigeons ate off of me, and descending the Euromast 328 feet on a rope.

—Jack Bell in *The New York Times*

In the recent Beangate case at Chipotle, *Maxim* editor Seth Porges started an e-mail **and Twitter campaign when he, a non-pork eater "for religious and cultural reasons," discovered that for the past 10 years he had been getting bacon along with the pinto beans in his burrito.**

—Joe Yonan in *The Washington Post*

Enormity

✦ **What's the Trouble?** **Enormity** is often used to mean "enormousness," but some people think that's an error.

Enormity is regularly used to describe something of staggering hugeness, but *enormousness* means the same thing, and some people (including some respected usage guide writers) think *enormity* should be reserved to mean something akin to "atrociousness" or "wickedness."

Garner's Modern American Usage seems to (grudgingly) give up the fight on *enormity,* and *Merriam-Webster's Dictionary of English Usage* (*MWDEU*) makes a compelling argument for allowing *enormity* to describe a vast immensity. Besides highlighting a large number of examples from the 1800s to today of writers actually using *enormity* in the "prohibited" way, the *MWDEU* editors explain that there is no historical basis for the distinction. Nevertheless, *The Chicago Manual of Style* and *Strunk & White* want you to stick with *enormousness*.

What Should You Do?

Avoid ambiguity by avoiding *enormity* in contexts where the meaning could be either "huge" or "horrible."

Unless you're required to follow a style guide that favors *enormousness,* use *enormity* to mean "hugeness" with only a twinge of fear. Although *enormity* will sound more natural than *enormousness* to most readers, a cadre of people still exist who will think you've broken a rule. Only you can decide when the risk is worth taking.

> **The date itself [September 11] is a loaded term that evokes the enormousness, and the** enormity, **of the deed that redefined our times.**
>
> —A Canadian *Chronicle Herald* editorial

Entitled

✦ What's the Trouble? Both **entitled** and *titled* can mean "having the title of . . ."

Webster's Collegiate Dictionary and *The American Heritage Dictionary of the English Language* list *entitle* and *title* as synonyms when they are used as verbs: they both indicate that something is being given a title.

Entitled can also be used to indicate that people have a certain right (such as the right to an opinion) or feel a sense of entitlement (that they are due something).

What Should You Do?

Although *entitled* isn't incorrect, stick with *titled* when you're referring to a title.

> **EMD Serono, a biopharmaceutical company, has produced a campaign on Facebook** titled **"Birds and the Bees: The Real Story." Part of the campaign features a music video, "Early Bird Catches the Sperm," reminiscent of a digital short on "Saturday Night Live."**
>
> —Jessica Ryen Doyle on *Fox News*

> **Dr. Niles Crane: [Maris] drove up on the sidewalk, and when the police ran her name through the computer, they found quite a little backlog of unpaid parking tickets.**
>
> **Dr. Frasier Crane: What else would you expect from a woman who thinks her chocolate allergy** entitles **her to park in a handicapped space?**
>
> —David Hyde Pierce as Niles and Kelsey Grammer as Frasier in the TV series *Frasier*

Fish

✦ What's the Trouble? **Fish** has two acceptable plural forms: *fish* and *fishes*.

Fish is the most common plural form of *fish*, but there are some instances in which people use *fishes*. Scientists who study *fish* (ichthyologists) for example, often refer to different species as *fishes*. In the biblical book of Mark, Jesus feeds thousands of men the *five loaves and two fishes*. Finally, the movie *The Godfather* popularized the phrase *sleeps with the fishes* to describe mob killings in which a corpse is dumped in the water.

What Should You Do?

Use *fish* as the plural of *fish* unless you're writing about biology or making references to *The Godfather* or the Bible.

> **[Tessio brings in Luca Brasi's bulletproof vest, delivered with a fish inside]**
>
> **SONNY: What the hell is this?**
>
> **CLEMENZA: It's a Sicilian message. It means Luca Brasi sleeps with the** fishes.
>
> —Richard Castellano as Clemenza and James Caan as Sonny in the movie *The Godfather*

> **The pike is one of the few** fishes **with binocular sight; both eyes look forward and the visual fields overlap.**
>
> —Len Cacutt in *Fishes*

> **When you go fishing you can catch a lot of** fish, **or you can catch a big** fish. **You ever walk into a guy's den and see a picture of him standing next to fourteen trout?**
>
> —Justin Timberlake as Sean Parker in the movie *The Social Network*

Flaunt

+ What's the Trouble? People sometimes confuse **flaunt** and *flout*.

Flaunt and *flout* sound similar but don't mean the same thing. When you flaunt yourself, your wealth, or accomplishments, you're parading them in front of people—showing off. *Flout* means "to disregard, scoff at, mock, or show scorn." A rebel flouts rules and laws.

What Should You Do?

Remember that *flaunt* means "to show off" and *flout* means to "disregard."

> ### QUICK AND DIRTY TIP
>
> Remember that you *flout laws* by linking the *out* in *flout* with the idea of being <u>out</u>side society.

That's it, baby! When you got it, flaunt **it,** flaunt **it!**

—Nathan Lane as Max Bialystock in the movie
The Producers

The [flapper] asserted her right to dance, drink, smoke, and date . . . to live free of the strictures that governed her mother's generation. . . . She flouted **Victorian-era conventions and scandalized her parents.**

—Joshua Zeitz in *Flapper: A Madcap Story of Sex, Style, Celebrity, and the Women Who Made America Modern*

Flier

✦ What's the Trouble? People aren't sure whether papers with information, or "handbills," are **fliers** or flyers.

Supposedly, *flier* is the American spelling and *flyer* is the British spelling. That's what *Garner's Modern American Usage* claims, and that claim is backed up by the Associated Press (an American organization), which recommends *flier*, and *The Economist* (a British publication), which recommends *flyer*.

On the other hand, when addressing the "handbill" meaning, *Webster's Third* (an American dictionary) says the word is usually spelled *flyer*, and the *Oxford English Dictionary* (a dictionary with British roots), says the U.S. spelling is *flyer*. A Google Books Ngram search (which isn't restricted by meaning) shows that *flyer* is more common than *flier* in both British English and American English and that both spellings have coexisted since at least 1800.

What Should You Do?

If you're following Associated Press style, use *flier* to mean "handbill." Otherwise, pick the spelling you prefer and use it consistently.

> **We're barely making enough to survive, with no hope for anything better. I couldn't dream anymore about school. But when I saw this** flier**, I felt life getting back into me.**
> —Mackenzie Astin as Will Stoneman in the movie *Iron Will*

Flyer seems to be preferred in the names of buses and trains such as the Midnight Flyer, and *flier* seems to be preferred when you mean "one who flies," but it's easy to find exceptions.

For Free

+ **What's the Trouble? For free** is common, but some usage experts disparage it.

Typically, *for* is followed by an amount: *You can have that teacup* ***for five dollars****. I'll give you that saucer* ***for nothing****. Free* isn't an amount; it's a description that means "without charge" or "without cost." You could answer the question *How much do you have?* by responding, *Five dollars,* or *Nothing,* but not by responding *Free.*

Nevertheless, *for free* is so common that some people consider it an idiom, and there are instances in which you can't swap *free* and *for free* without making your sentence sound awkward or causing confusion.

> **Kevin Williams can't wait to get out on to the field with his Minnesota Vikings teammates for the first time this season after missing the first two games because of a suspension.**
>
> **He's a little less excited about playing the next two games** for free.
>
> [*Free* alone could have been confusing, perhaps suggesting that he is a free agent. W*ithout pay* could be a better choice.]
>
> —Jon Krawczynski writing for the Associated Press
>
> **We're not going to break anything. Don't think of it as breaking into SeaWorld. Think of it as visiting SeaWorld in the middle of the night** for free.

[*Free* alone would be awkward since it is at such a distance from what it is modifying: *visiting*. The sentence could be fixed by writing *Think of it as a free visit to Sea-World in the middle of the night*.]

—John Green in *Paper Towns*

What Should You Do?

The instances in which you simply can't drop the *for* from *for free* are rare, and *for free* still draws enough negative attention that it's worth the extra effort to rewrite your sentences to avoid it.

Free Gift

✦ **What's the Trouble? Free gift** is usually redundant.

Gifts should be free by definition, right? It's rarely necessary to write about a free gift. *Gift* alone should suffice.

On the other hand, although it's redundant, *free gift* is so common in advertisements that it's hard to call it an error. Let's just say that it should be limited to the domain of advertisers because they seem to find it effective.

What Should You Do?

Avoid the phrase *free gift* unless you're writing ads.

> **So speak up, America. Speak up for the home of the brave. Speak up for the land of the** free gift **with purchase!**
>
> —Reese Witherspoon as Elle Woods in the movie
> *Legally Blonde 2: Red, White & Blonde*

Fun

✦ **What's the Trouble?** Some people think **fun** can't be used as an adjective and other people think it's fine to use *funnest*.

Fun often means something different depending on how old you are—both literally and linguistically. Literally, an eighty-year-old may find fun in a crossword puzzle, whereas an eight-year-old may crave a roller coaster ride. Linguistically, everyone agrees that *fun* is a noun (e.g., *everyone had fun*), but older people think the fun stops there, whereas younger people think *fun* can also be an adjective (e.g., *it was a fun party*).

Although *fun* has been used as an adjective since the mid-1800s, there was a burst of talk about *fun cars, fun clothes, fun parties,* and *fun people* starting right after World War II and the use continued on. More than one language expert has commented on the link between age and how acceptable people find *fun,* the adjective.

One argument against allowing *fun* to be used as an adjective is that the comparative and superlative forms (*funner* and *funnest*) are still considered objectionable (or at least wildly informal) by almost everyone, and it's a problem to have an adjective that can't take the same normal extended forms as other adjectives.

Fun

What Should You Do?

Feel free to use *fun* as an adjective unless you're writing for a publication whose audience is largely older readers. Avoid *funner* and *funnest* unless you're trying to sound like a dude or dudette. (Or a revered tech CEO. Don't forget that Steve Jobs introduced the new iPod Touch in 2008 by calling it the "*funnest* iPod ever.")

If you never did you should. These things are fun and fun is good.

[*fun* as a predicate adjective and a noun]

—Dr. Seuss in *One Fish Two Fish Red Fish Blue Fish*

A Supposedly Fun Thing I'll Never Do Again

[*fun* as an adjective]

—Title of a David Foster Wallace book of essays and arguments

You wanna talk fun? Public bus. You meet the funnest people.

[*funnest* as the superlative of fun]

—Nicholas Brendon as Xander in the TV series *Buffy the Vampire Slayer*

Gauntlet

✦ **What's the Trouble?** Many style guides recommend *gantlet* in the phrase most people write as *run the* **gauntlet**.

Many usage experts say *gauntlet* and *gantlet* have different origins and that a *gauntlet* is only a glove and a *gantlet* is only a path lined with attackers. Therefore, you throw down the *gauntlet* (glove) to challenge someone and pick up the *gauntlet* (glove) to accept a challenge, but you run the *gantlet* (a course).

Most style guides still support the distinction. For example, the *AP Stylebook* currently recommends using *gantlet* in phrases such as *run the gantlet*. However, in the past, the AP editors have said they bow to common usage (for example, when they changed their recommendation from *e-mail* to *email*). They are likely to abandon the *gantlet* requirement in the near future, particularly because two large newspapers have reported receiving significant mail chiding them for the "error" when they have used *gantlet* as AP recommends. Further, *run the gauntlet* already appears more often in books than *run the gantlet*.

Finally, *Merriam-Webster's Dictionary of English Usage* digs into the etymology of *gauntlet* and finds that the distinction from *gantlet* is not so clear. Although they are usually pronounced differently now, early on *gantlet* and *gauntlet* were simply variant spellings of the Swedish word *gatalopp*, which meant "road" or "course" and was making its way into English. They find no reason *gantlet* became the preferred spelling, and if fact, suggest it may be because of their own distinction between the words in one of their early dictionaries, which they regret.

Gauntlet

What Should You Do?

Unless you're following a style guide that requires *gantlet*, use *gauntlet* when you're talking about running down a lane while being attacked. If you use *gantlet*, you run a significant risk of being viewed as incorrect or precious.

> **Tom Paris: When you said "Be there in a minute," you weren't kidding.**
>
> **B'Elanna Torres: A group of Klingons ambushed me outside of Engineering. I decided transporting myself would be easier than running the** gauntlet.
>
> —Robert Duncan McNeill as Tom Paris and Roxann
> Dawson as B'Elanna Torres in the TV series
> *Star Trek: Voyager*

Gender

✦ **What's the Trouble?** **Gender** has become a questionable replacement for *sex*.

People often use the word *gender* as a "delicate" way to ask someone's sex, but it's technically something else. When you ask what someone's sex is, you're asking whether they have the physical characteristics of a male or a female. *Gender* is a social construct, so when you ask someone's gender, you're asking whether a person wants to be perceived as what society calls male or society calls female. That's why *inter**sex*** is used to describe someone who has both male and female physical characteristics, and *trans**gender*** is used to describe people who are physically male but present themselves to the world as if they are female, and vice versa.

What Should You Do?

If your readers are likely to be extremely squeamish about sex, it's OK to use *gender* as a replacement for *sex,* but if not, try to keep the distinction between the two words.

> **Ted you may wanna find a new** gender **for yourself 'cause I'm revoking your dude membership.**
>
> —Neil Patrick Harris as Barney in the TV series
> *How I Met Your Mother*

> **There are two types of male oysters, and one of them can change** genders **at will.**
>
> [*Sex* would have been a better choice since, presumably, oysters have no culture that defines social constructs such as *gender.*]
>
> —William Petersen as Gil Grissom in the TV series
> *CSI: Crime Scene Investigation*

Gone Missing

✦ **What's the Trouble?** Many Americans find **gone missing** annoying, yet it is not incorrect.

Gone missing is a Britishism that has made its way to the United States, where it is primarily used by journalists to describe missing persons. Although reporters and newscasters seem to love *gone missing,* it's easy to find vocal readers and viewers who hate it.

Haters argue that a person must go to a location, and *missing* isn't a place, and that an inanimate object can't go missing because it can't take action alone—but English has never been so literal. In a tight labor market, jobs can go begging (be unfilled), for example, even though *begging* is not a location and jobs can't take action. Other peevers suggest that *gone missing* necessitates an action on the part of the person or item that has vanished. Again, we have parallels that undermine the argument: Milk goes bad, for example, without taking any action on its own.

Gone missing is not wrong. The *Oxford English Dictionary* places it in the same category as the phrase *go native,* as in *We had high hopes for our new senator, but after he was in Washington for a few months he went native.*

What Should You Do?

If *gone missing* bothers you, use a word such as *disappeared* in your own writing. You can criticize *gone missing* as annoying if you like, but not as incorrect.

Gone Missing

The sheriff of Area 9 in Texas has gone missing. **He is twice as old as I am and very powerful. If one such as he can be taken, than none of us is safe.**

> —Alexander Skarsgård as Eric Northman in the
> TV series *True Blood*

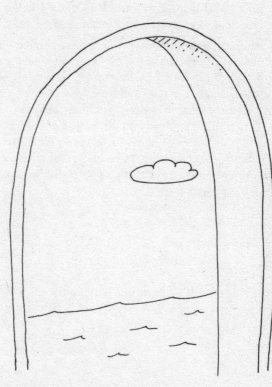

Gotten

✦ **What's the Trouble?** In the past, some schoolbooks taught that **gotten** is incorrect as the past participle of the verb *to get,* but such advice has a dubious source.

The British rarely use *gotten* as the past participle of *get* anymore (they prefer *got*), but it's still the most common American form and is accepted by major American style guides. British style guides disparaged *gotten* back in the 1800s and that criticism made its way into some popular American schoolbooks.

Although *gotten* is fine in America, we also use *got. Merriam-Webster's Dictionary of English Usage* says Americans use *gotten* and *got* "in a way that is almost freely variable." However, which word you use can change the meaning of some sentences. *Got* can have a sense of ownership, whereas *gotten* can have a sense of process. *The American Heritage Guide to Contemporary Usage and Style* highlights it best with these two examples: *I haven't got any money* (which says you're broke) versus *I haven't gotten any money* (which says you haven't been paid).

(Also see *Have Got*.)

What Should You Do?

Don't be afraid to use *gotten*, but in sentences where *got* could mean something different, be sure you choose the right word.

> **The photograph caught four black bears as they puzzled over a suspended food bag. The bears were clearly startled but not remotely alarmed by the flash. It was not the size or demeanor of the bears that troubled me—they looked almost comically nonaggressive, like four guys who had** gotten **a Frisbee caught up a tree—but their numbers. Up to that moment it had not occurred to me that bears might prowl in parties.**
>
> —Bill Bryson in *A Walk in the Woods: Rediscovering America on the Appalachian Trail*

Graduated

✦ **What's the Trouble?** People are starting to drop the *from* in sentences such as *Johnny* **graduated** *from high school*.

Seventy years ago, parents said *Johnny was graduated from high school,* but that's a passive construction. By the mid-1960s, people had dropped the *was,* and the active form had become the standard form: *Johnny graduated from high school.* Recently, *graduated* has been the target of another change: people are starting to drop the *from* and simply say *Johnny graduated high school.*

The new, shorter form may eventually become standard, but it's currently considered wrong because a school does the act of graduating and the new way of saying it seems to imply that Johnny did the act of graduating.

What Should You Do?

Stick with the *graduated from* construction: *Johnny graduated from high school.*

> **[phone rings]**
>
> **CLIFF: Oh, not another Vanessa caller.**
>
> **[answers]**
>
> **CLIFF: Vanessa's Residence? . . . No, she cannot come to the phone right now. . . . Because it is now 10:05, and she cannot take any calls past 10 o'clock. . . . No, I cannot take a message. I am her father. I am a doctor. I** graduated **from medical school, all right?**
>
> —Bill Cosby as Heathcliff Huxtable in the TV series
> *The Cosby Show*

Grow

✦ **What's the Trouble?** Some people object to using **grow** with intangible objects (e.g., *grow the economy* instead of *grow roses*).

Clearly, *grow* can take an object. People have been growing rice and wheat for millennia. People have only spoken of growing investments or economies for a few decades though, and outside of business circles, using such nonorganic, intangible objects with the transitive verb *grow* raises some eyebrows.

Nevertheless, metaphorically, investments and economies need tending in the same way that plants need water and fertilizer.

What Should You Do?

Grow in this sense is firmly established in business writing and isn't going away. Freely use *grow* with nonliving things in business publications, but be more hesitant in other types of publications.

> **Voters next fall may be able to weigh two strongly contrasting views of how to** grow **the economy and create jobs.**
>
> —*Christian Science Monitor* editorial board

NOTE: Odd as it may seem, it's perfectly acceptable to say something *grew smaller*. "Become" has long been one of the definitions of *grow*.

Half

✦ What's the Trouble? **Half** can be singular or plural.

Typically, subjects and verbs must agree: If the subject is singular, the verb is singular, and if the subject is plural, the verb is plural. However, sentences that start with *half* don't follow this rule.

Half alone is singular, but although *half* is the subject in a sentence such as *Half the boys are missing,* we use a plural verb because of something called notional agreement. It simply means that although *half* is singular, the subject has a notion of being plural, so the plural verb is OK.

Half has a few other quirks too. Compound words that start with *half* can be open, closed, or hyphenated (e.g., *half note, halfhearted, half-baked*). There's no rule, so you have to check a dictionary. And although *half of* isn't wrong, usually the meaning doesn't change and your sentence is more concise if you leave out the *of*.

What Should You Do?

Follow this rule when *half* is the subject of a sentence: If *half* is followed by a singular noun, use a singular verb. If *half* is followed by a plural noun, use a plural verb.

> Half **the world** is **composed of people who have something to say and can't, and the other half who have nothing to say and keep on saying it.**
>
> —Robert Frost, American poet

> Half **of the American people** have **never read a newspaper. Half never voted for President. One hopes it is the same half.**
>
> —Gore Vidal, American fiction and nonfiction writer

Hanukkah

✦ What's the Trouble? There are many acceptable ways to spell **Hanukkah**.

The Jewish holiday also known as the Festival of Lights can be spelled *Chanukah, Hanukkah, Hanukah,* and *Hannukah*. And that's just the beginning. Hebrew words like *Hanukkah* can't be directly translated to English because English and Hebrew use different alphabets. Instead, words are transliterated: given English spellings based on how they are pronounced. Transliteration leaves spelling open to interpretation.

The most popular spelling in the Corpus of Contemporary American English (a huge database of English text) is *Hanukkah,* and that is also the spelling recommended by the Associated Press.

What Should You Do?

Pick one spelling and use it consistently. *Hanukkah* is a good example of why organizations need style guides.

> **Some nights, some places are a little brighter. It's difficult to stare at New York City on Valentine's Day, or Dublin on St. Patrick's. The old walled city of Jerusalem lights up like a candle on each of** Chanukah's **eight nights . . . *We're here*, the glow . . . will say in one and a half centuries. *We're here, and we're alive*.**
>
> —Jonathan Safran Foer in *Everything Is Illuminated*

Have Got

✦ **What's the Trouble?** Some people say that *got* is unnec-
essary and incorrect when inserted between *have to* in
sentences such as *You* **have got** *to see my new parrot*.

Got, indeed, does not not significantly change the meaning
when it's included after the helping verb *have* (*I have to buy
some birdseed* versus *I have got to buy some birdseed*). It does,
however, add emphasis, just as *myself* adds emphasis in a sentence such as *I picked out the parrot myself*.

Have got has been used in English for centuries and is considered fully standard by most modern usage guides.

What Should You Do?

Use *have got to* without fear when your sentence merits extra
emphasis.

> **If you have anything to say, anything you feel
> nobody has ever said before, you** have got **to
> feel it so desperately that you will find some
> way to say it that nobody has ever found
> before, so that the thing you have to say and
> the way of saying it blend as one matter—
> as indissolubly as if they were conceived
> together.**

> —F. Scott Fitzgerald in *The Short Stories
> of F. Scott Fitzgerald*

Healthy

✦ **What's the Trouble?** Some people insist that carrots aren't **healthy**; they're *healthful* because only *healthful* can mean "conducive to health."

Healthy has long been used to describe things that improve your constitution. *Healthful* gained ground against *healthy* starting in the late 1800s, but *healthy* fought back and now, although *healthful* isn't wrong, *healthy* is the dominant Standard English word we use when describing fruits, vegetables, exercise, and other things we hope will make us live longer.

What Should You Do?

Ignore anyone who says you have to use *healthful* instead of *healthy* (unless you're trying to feign an "old-timey" air).

It's a very healthful **drink! Even better for you than placing leeches on your tongue.**

—Gary Coleman voicing Kenny Falmouth in the video game *The Curse of Monkey Island*

Hero

✦ **What's the Trouble?** **Hero** is overused and misunderstood.

Some dictionaries include a definition of *hero* that means "an admired person," but readers can object when writers extend the *hero* label to an entire class of people (e.g., all firefighters or all soldiers) or people who are just doing a difficult job (e.g., an excellent teacher). Such readers maintain that a person must do something extraordinary to be a hero—that there may be heroes among firefighters, but not every firefighter is heroic; and that people must accomplish more than simply doing their job well to be a hero.

Hero also has other meanings. For example, in literature, a *hero* can be simply "the main character in a work," and in classic mythology, a *hero* is "a strong, courageous man who may have godlike powers or be favored by the gods."

What Should You Do?

Although it's not incorrect to use *hero* to describe someone you admire or think your readers should admire, consider whether a different description may be more appropriate or less grating to certain readers.

> **[Homer has been thrown out of an all-you-can-eat restaurant for eating too much]**
>
> **Lionel Hutz: This is the most blatant case of false advertising since my suit against the movie *The NeverEnding Story*.**

HOMER: So, do you think I have a case?

**LIONEL HUTZ: Mr. Simpson, I don't use the word
"hero" lightly, but you are the greatest** hero
in American history.

HOMER: Woohoo!

—Phil Hartman voicing Lionel and Dan Castellaneta
voicing Homer in the TV series *The Simpsons*

Hopefully

✦ **What's the Trouble?** Although it's common to use **hopefully** to mean "I hope," many people object to such use.

For centuries, *hopefully* meant "in a hopeful manner."

> **To travel** hopefully **is a better thing than to arrive.**
>
> —Scottish writer Robert Louis Stevenson

In the 1960s, people started using *hopefully* to mean "I hope" or "we hope." It became trendy. At the time, usage experts objected to the new meaning, but those objections failed to stick. Today, *hopefully* to mean "I hope" is widespread and most style guides have softened their stance. *Merriam-Webster's Dictionary of English Usage* pins the peak of *hopefully* opposition to 1975; nevertheless, many people are still alive today who remember the early and more vehement opposition.

> **TREY ATWOOD: Ryan said you talk a lot.**
>
> **SETH: Yeah, it's kind of a problem but** hopefully **one you'll come to find endearing.**
>
> —Logan Marshall-Green as Trey and Adam Brody as Seth in the TV series *The O.C*

What Should You Do?

Hide under a rock? Unfortunately, you can't win with *hopefully*. Although the arguments against using it as a sentence adverb are uncompelling (it's not much different from *frankly* and *thankfully*), and it commonly appears in print and everyday language, you are still quite likely to draw criticism from a large pool of objectors if you use it. Take comfort in the knowledge it probably won't be a problem for your children.

I'd've

✦ **What's the Trouble?** Some contractions that mimic speech patterns seem odd in writing.

When we speak, we often slur and contract our words. Some of these contractions are also common in print (*there's, I'm*), yet others look unusual and awkward (**I'd've**, *that've, there're*). *I'd've* is no less correct than *should've,* and *there're* is no less correct than *there's*, but using such odd contractions could throw your readers.

What Should You Do?

Unless you're going for an informal, breezy air that closely mimics speech, avoid the less common contractions such as *I'd've.*

> **Newt did something graceful. Karen Tumulty, I believe, said "Congressman Gingrich," then corrected herself with "Speaker Gingrich." And Newt broke in, "Newt." (If I had been the reporter, I'd've said "Mr. Gingrich." I don't think these titles should carry on forever.)**
>
> —Jay Nordlinger in his "Impromptus" column for the *National Review Online*

Into

✦ **What's the Trouble?** Determining whether you need **into** or *in to* can be tricky.

Into indicates motion, and *in* indicates position: *You accidentally walked into a wall, and you were in your room when the phone rang.* That seems simple enough.

The tricky part is that *in* is also part of phrasal verbs such as *tune in, opt in,* and *log in* that can just happen to come before *to* in a sentence. That's when you have to be careful. For example, you <u>tune in</u> to a radio station; you don't tune <u>into</u> it.

What Should You Do?

When you're not sure whether to use *into* or *in to,* ask yourself whether there is motion (if so, you usually want *into*), or whether your verb would have a different meaning if you deleted the word *in* (if so, you usually want *in to*).

> **TMZ has video of [Shia] LaBeouf being punched by an unnamed person while laying on the ground. Others outside quickly stepped in to pull Shia out of there.**

[Note that *stepped* has a different meaning than *stepped in.*]

—Charley Been writing for *StarzLife*

> **[R]eplacing departed star Shia LaBeouf with Brit muscleman Jason Statham could inject some new testosterone-driven energy into the series.**

[Note that *inject into* indicates metaphorical motion—energy flowing into the series.]

—Dave Lewis writing for *HitFix*

It Is I

✦ **What's the Trouble?** **It is I** is technically correct, but most people say *It is me*.

Grammatically, *I* is the correct choice following a linking verb such as *is*, meaning when people ask *Who is there?* you should answer *It is I*. Nevertheless, to most people, *It is I* sounds overly formal even after they are taught the rule.

It's not a modern problem. Back in 1878, Henry Alford, the Dean of Canterbury and author of a popular usage book of the era, *A Plea for the Queen's English*, called *It is me* a "well known and much controverted phrase." He defended *It is me*, saying, "This is an expression that everyone uses. Grammarians (of the smaller order) protest; schoolmasters (of the lower kind) prohibit and chastise; but English men, women, and children go on saying it, and will go on saying it as long as the English language is spoken."

Modern usage guides continue to support *It is me*.

What Should You Do?

In all but the most formal situations, feel free to use *It is me* or *It's me*.

It is I; be not afraid.

—Jesus in the book of Matthew

***Are You There God?* It's Me, Margaret.**

—Judy Blume book title

Jealous

✦ What's the Trouble? Jealous and *envious* have overlapping meanings and are often used interchangeably.

Some sources say *jealous* should be limited to resentful emotional rivalries (often romantic) with another person, whereas *envious* can expand to cover desiring or coveting the objects or accomplishments of another person. Jealousy can also come with an element of fear that you might lose someone, whereas if you are envious, you simply want what somebody else has.

For example, maybe you're jealous of your girlfriend's best friend who's a dude, but you're envious of her upcoming trip to Hawaii. If she's going to Hawaii with the dude, you can be jealous and envious at the same time! (Clearly, it's a doomed relationship.)

Nevertheless, *jealous* is commonly used in movies and magazine articles when *envious* would be the more precise term according to traditional definitions, and dictionaries include overlapping definitions. The distinction between the two words in practice is weak, at best.

What Should You Do?

If you wish to be precise, make a distinction between *jealous* and *envious* in your writing, but don't be surprised when the definitions are blurred in pop culture.

> **You people make me** envy **the deaf and the blind!**
>
> —Johnny Hardwick as Dale in the TV series *King of the Hill*

> **Oh, please. You can't tell me you weren't** jealous **that Vaughn had his hippie hands all over your debate-slash-make-out partner.**
>
> —Gillian Jacobs as Britta in the TV series *Community*

Kinds

✦ **What's the Trouble?** *Kind* slips in when people mean **kinds**.

You have one *kind* of peanut butter but three *kinds* of jelly. Use the singular (*kind*) when you have one of something; use the plural (*kinds*) when you have more. Since *these* and *those* indicate multiple things, you have to use a plural: *kinds*: *These kinds of situations always perplex me.* (*These kind of situations* is wrong.)

What Should You Do?

The best you can do is to watch out for the problem. Remember: when you have a plural adjective such as *these* or *those*, you need a plural noun, *kinds*: *Those kinds of restaurants always seem to fill up fast.*

> **The character strengths that enabled [Dominic Randolph] to achieve the success that he has were not built in his years at Harvard or at the boarding schools he attended; they came out of those years of trial and error, of taking chances and living without a safety net. And it is precisely those** kinds **of experiences that he worries that his students aren't having.**
>
> —Paul Tough in *The New York Times*

Kudos

✦ **What's the Trouble?** Some people mistakenly believe **kudos** is plural.

Kudos means "praise" or "glory" and is often used where "congratulations" would fit. It comes directly from Greek and is singular, just as *praise* and *glory* are singular. However, because *kudos* ends in *s* and *congratulations* is plural, some people mistakenly believe that *kudos* is plural and use *kudo* as a singular form. Such use is incorrect.

What Should You Do?

Use *kudos,* and remember that it's singular.

> **"I see that you are working this vampire angle with some success," Jace said, indicating Isabelle and Maia with a nod of his head. "And** kudos**. Lots of girls love that sensitive-undead thing. But I'd drop that whole musician angle if I were you. Vampire rock stars are played out, and besides, you can't possibly be very good."**
>
> —Cassandra Clare in *City of Glass*

> **Memo to self:** Kudos **are in order. I could win a Nobel Prize. If they ever add that Atrocities category.** [It should be *kudos is in order* or *congratulations are in order.*]
>
> —Alan Rachins as Professor Jefferson Cole in the TV series *Lois & Clark: The New Adventures of Superman*

Lay

✦ What's the Trouble? Lay is commonly used when *lie* is the right choice.

Bryan Garner, author of *Garner's Modern American Usage*, calls mistaking *lay* for *lie* "one of the most widely known of all usage errors," and *lay versus lie* is one of the top searches that brings people to the *Grammar Girl* website. Clearly, there's some confusion.

What Should You Do?

The rule is actually quite simple. *Lay* is the transitive verb (you use it when you are laying something down) and *lie* is the intransitive verb (you use it when you or someone you are describing is taking the action of lying down). You *lay a pen on the table*, and *lie down to sleep*.

> **I enjoy having breakfast in bed. I like waking up to the smell of bacon, sue me. And since I don't have a butler, I have to do it myself. So, most nights before I go to bed, I will** lay **six strips of bacon out on my George Foreman grill. Then I go to sleep. When I wake up, I plug in the grill. I go back to sleep again. Then I wake up to the smell of crackling bacon.**
>
> —Steve Carell as Michael Scott in the TV series *The Office*

Lighted and Lit

✦ **What's the Trouble?** The verb *to light* has two acceptable past tense forms.

Odd as it may seem, both **lighted** and **lit** are equally acceptable past tense forms of the verb *to light*.

Lighted is a regular form (because you add *-ed* to the end to make it past tense), and *lit* is an irregular form (because you change the spelling instead of adding *-ed* to the end), but irregular does not mean less acceptable. In fact, *lit* appears more often in print than *lighted*.

- **I lighted three candles.**
- **I lit three candles.**

Lighted is the older adjective form according to the *Oxford English Dictionary*, but again, both *lighted* and *lit* are standard adjectives.

- **He saw her across the lighted ballroom.**
- **He saw her across the lit ballroom.**

What Should You Do?

Choose whichever word sounds better in your sentence.

> **Thousands of candles can be** lighted/lit **from a single candle, and the life of the candle will not be shortened. Happiness never decreases by being shared.**
>
> —A Buddhist saying that appears in both forms

Media

✦ **What's the Trouble? Media** is treated as both singular and plural.

Media comes from Latin, in which *medium* is the singular and *media* is the plural. However, foreign words can change their stripes when they become rooted in English, and *media* is doing just that.

In English, *media* is often used as a collective noun like *band* or *team,* and in America we usually treat collective nouns as singular nouns: *The band is here, the team is excited,* and *the media is on the story.* (In Britain, collective nouns are usually treated as plural.)

What Should You Do?

When *media* is used as a collective noun, it's fine to use a singular verb. The *AP Stylebook* and *The Chicago Manual of Style* support such use, although it's not unheard of for an American editor to favor using a plural verb. You'll see *the media are,* but you'll see *the media is* more often:

> **Whoa, this really beats the pressure of playing big league ball, there if you make a mistake, and "boom" the** media **is all over you.**
>
> —Major League Baseball catcher Mike Scioscia as himself in the TV series *The Simpsons*

> **As anybody who has read a newspaper since 1788 will know, the British** media **are somewhat obsessed with London, at the expense of everywhere else.**
>
> —Scott Murray writing for *The Guardian*

Momentarily

✦ What's the Trouble? **Momentarily** is losing its original meaning.

Momentarily has its roots in the word *momentary*—as in the Pink Floyd album *A Momentary Lapse of Reason*—and it traditionally means "for a moment." However, it's more common nowadays to hear people use *momentarily* when they mean "in a moment." The *Oxford English Dictionary* says this is mainly an American problem.

What Should You Do?

Don't use *momentarily* to mean "for a moment"; you may confuse people. If you mean *in a moment,* say or write that. There's no need to use *momentarily* in such cases, and doing so will irritate language purists.

> **Tom Scavo:** [Lynette is sitting at her computer] **What're you doing?**
>
> **Lynette Scavo:** I'm just talking to Porter on Silverfizz.
>
> **Tom Scavo:** Who is Sarah J from MacArthur High School?
>
> **Lynette Scavo:** Me! I'm sixteen, cute, I like graphic novels and Tokyo Police Club.
>
> **Tom Scavo:** Oh my God! You're pretending to be somebody else!
>
> **Lynette Scavo:** Our brooding son has a classmate who got arrested for selling drugs, I really think the ends justify the means.

Tom Scavo: We'll address your major ethical breach in a moment. **What did you find out?**

> —Doug Savant as Tom Scavo and Felicity Huffman as Lynette Scavo in the TV series *Desperate Housewives*

Dr. Rodney McKay: I figured out a way to create a glitch that, on my command, should momentarily **freeze them.**

Ronon Dex: How long?

Dr. Rodney McKay: Well, I don't know. That's why I said "momentarily."

> —David Hewlett as McKay and Jason Momoa as Dex in the TV series *Stargate: Atlantis*

Myriad

✦ What's the Trouble? Some sources say the phrase *a myriad of* is unacceptable; others say it's fine.

The American Heritage Guide to Contemporary Usage and Style notes that using *myriad* as a noun (e.g., *a myriad of*) has been common throughout most of English history, and it was only in the early nineteenth century that *myriad* started to be used as an adjective (e.g., *in myriad ways*), and at first only poetically. Other respectable style guides agree that *a myriad of* is fine, but the Associated Press instructs its writers thus in the entry on *myriad*: "word is not followed by *of*." Therefore, writers who are familiar only with AP style can believe the phrase *a myriad of* is wrong.

> **Cheese covers a** myriad **of sins.**
>
> —Jessica Biel as Mary in the TV series *7th Heaven*

> **Books grant us** myriad **possibilities: the possibility of change, the possibility of illumination.**
>
> —Alberto Manguel in *The Library at Night*

The plural noun, *myriads* is also allowed by some—in the sense of a huge amount such as tens of thousands—and frowned upon by others.

> **One of the proofs of the immortality of the soul is that** myriads **have believed it. They also believed the world was flat.**
>
> —Mark Twain

What Should You Do?

Freely use *a myriad of* unless you follow AP style, but know that you may occasionally get complaints when you do so.

Neither...Nor

✦ **What's the Trouble?** Choosing a singular or plural verb can be tricky when writing a **neither . . . nor** sentence.

People often seem incorrectly drawn to plural verbs when writing with *neither* and *nor*. However, *neither* and *nor* create something called an "alternate subject," which means you use the closest noun or pronoun to choose your verb.

- **singular** + **plural** = **plural verb** (*Neither milk nor cookies are on the menu.*)
- **plural** + **singular** = **singular verb** (*Neither cookies nor milk is on the menu.*)
- **plural** + **plural** = **plural verb** (*Neither brownies nor cookies are on the menu.*)
- **singular** + **singular** = **singular verb** (*Neither milk nor orange juice is on the menu.*)

The same rules apply for *either . . . or* constructions.

What Should You Do?

Remember that the noun closest to the verb drives your verb choice. Also, it's better to put the plural verb last if possible.

> **Neither love** nor **evil conquers all, but evil cheats more.**
>
> [singular (*love*) + singular (*evil*) = singular verb (*conquers*)]
>
> —Laurell K. Hamilton in *Cerulean Sins*

Next

✦ What's the Trouble? People think **next** means different things when it modifies a day of the week.

Some people think *next Friday* means the next Friday that will occur, and other people think *next Friday* means the Friday in the next week, regardless of what day it is in the current week.

What Should You Do?

There is no definitive meaning for *next Friday*, and even if there were, using it would still cause confusion. Avoid using *next* to modify a day of the week. Be more specific.

> **SID: Well I'm going down to visit my sister in Virginia** next **Wednesday, for a week, so I can't park it.**
>
> **JERRY: This Wednesday?**
>
> **SID: No,** next **Wednesday, week after this Wednesday.**
>
> **JERRY: But the Wednesday two days from now is the** next **Wednesday.**
>
> **SID: If I meant this Wednesday, I would have said this Wednesday. It's the week after this Wednesday.**
>
> —Jerry Seinfeld as Jerry and Jay Brooks as Sid in the TV series *Seinfeld*

Noisome

✦ What's the Trouble? Noisome has nothing to do with noise.

Noisome sounds like *noisy*, but that's not what it means. A *noisome problem* offends your nose, not your ears. Noisome means "offensive or disgusting," but is used almost exclusively to describe smells.

What Should You Do?

Remember that *noisome* means "stinky," and don't use *noisome* in a sentence where a misinformed reader could interpret it to mean "noisy."

QUICK AND DIRTY TIP

Instead of focusing on the initial letters that mislead you to *noisy*, focus on the pronunciation. Noisome comes from the Middle English word for "annoy." Think of it as "annoy-some."

> **"Amsterdam," I say, "would be superb were it not for its stinks." Murray says, "There is a good deal of mud deposited at the bottom of the canals, which, when disturbed by barges, produces a most noisome effluvia when the water is said to 'grow.' Machines are constantly at work to clear out the mud, which is sent to distant parts as manure."**
>
> —J. Ashby-Sterry in *Tiny Travels*

None

+ **What's the Trouble?** **None** can be singular or plural, but many people think it can only be singular.

None usually means "not one" and is followed by a noun and a singular verb.

However, sometimes *none* means "not any" giving your sentence a sense of plurality. In such cases, *none* can take a plural verb.

> **You will find that I will only truly have left this school when** none **here are loyal to me.**
>
> —J. K. Rowling in *Harry Potter and the Chamber of Secrets*

What Should You Do?

You may be chided by the uninformed when you follow *none* with a plural verb, but don't be afraid to do so if it's clear your sentence calls for it.

Nevertheless, it's not as common for *none* to mean "not any" as it is for *none* to mean "not one," and it's easy to be mistakenly drawn to a plural verb when *none* is followed by a plural noun. If you're not certain and have to guess, go with a singular verb.

Odds

✦ **What's the Trouble?** Many people have trouble understanding **odds**.

Mathematically, *odds* and *probability* are not the same thing, although colloquially, many people treat the words as synonyms. Further complicating matters, odds for the same event can be presented in different ways. For example, one person may think of the odds of rolling a six on a regular six-sided die as 1 to 5 in favor, and another person may think of the odds as 5 to 1 against.

You can get in particular trouble when you talk about odds being high because *high odds* can mean "something is likely or unlikely" depending on how your reader interprets it. The same goes with *low odds*.

What Should You Do?

If you want to say that "something is likely," say *there's a good chance* or *a high probability* of it happening. If you must use *odds,* say they are *good odds* or *bad odds,* not "high" or "low" odds.

> **Happy Hunger Games! And may the** odds **be ever in your favor.**
>
> —Suzanne Collins in *The Hunger Games*

OK

✦ **What's the Trouble?** This well-known American affirmative has two acceptable spellings.

OK was born in America in the 1830s. Much like the text messaging abbreviations of today, *OK* was an abbreviation for a funny misspelling of *all correct*: *oll korrect*. According to the *Oxford English Dictionary*, the *okay* spelling didn't appear until 1895.

Today, both forms peacefully coexist. For example, the Associated Press recommends *OK* and *The Chicago Manual of Style* recommends *okay*.

What Should You Do?

If you work for someone else, use the spelling in your employer's recommended style guide.
If you're writing for yourself, pick your favorite spelling and use it consistently.

> **One out of four people in this country is mentally unbalanced. Think of your three closest friends; if they seem** OK, **then you're the one.**
>
> —Ann Landers, advice columnist

One

✦ **What's the Trouble?** **One** shows up in constructions such as *one in five* and *one of the people who,* which can be hard to pin down as singular or plural.

In a sentence such as *One-in-five people struggles with subject-verb agreement,* one is the subject and most style guides say the verb should be singular—it's driven by *one,* not *people.* (Dissenting authors suggest that when writers refer to *one-in-five people,* they usually don't mean "one single person"; they usually mean "20 percent of all people," which has a sense of being plural.)

In a sentence such as *One of the people who struggle with subject-verb agreement just threw a book out the window,* some style guides say *of the people who struggle with subject-verb agreement* is a phrase that needs to be internally consistent. In that phrase, *the people* drives the verb choice, making the verb plural. However, you'll find even more style guides that disagree with this rule than the previous one.

What Should You Do?

If you'd like a rule to follow, make the verb in your *one-in-five* sentences singular and the verb in your *one-of-the-people-who* sentences plural. However, the experts disagree so much about such cases that it's also fine to choose the verb that sounds best to you in your specific sentence.

> **Tell me, is it** one **in four marriages that end in divorce these days, or** one **in three?** [plural verb]
>
> —Renée Zellweger as Bridget in the movie
> *Bridget Jones's Diary*

According to the large survey by the European Committee in all EU Member States just **one** out of ten European citizens does not see climate change as a "serious problem." [singular verb]

—Rolf Schuttenhelm in *The Huffington Post*

Out Loud

✦ What's the Trouble? In days of old, *aloud* was the only cultured option.

In the early 1900s, usage guide writers looked down their noses at **out loud** and called it "colloquial." Today, *out loud* and *aloud* are both fine, although *aloud* still has a more high-brow or formal feel.

Context seems to drive people's preferences. *Read aloud* and *said aloud* are much more common in books than *read out loud* and *said out loud,* but *say it out loud* is more common than *say it aloud*; and not surprisingly, *laugh out loud* surpassed *laugh aloud* around 1975 and has been on a strong upward trend ever since.

What Should You Do?

Use whichever word sounds more natural to you, however, *aloud* is better for solemn or formal occasions such as asking someone to *read aloud* in church.

> **I thought such awful thoughts that I cannot even say them** out loud **because they would make Jesus want to drink gin straight out of the cat dish.**
>
> —Anne Lamott in *Traveling Mercies*

> **I was talking** aloud **to myself. A habit of the old: they choose the wisest person present to speak to.**
>
> —J. R. R. Tolkien in *The Two Towers*

Orientate

English has two verbs that mean the same thing: *orient* and **orientate**.

Orient is the older verb, but its rival, *orientate,* has been around since the mid-1800s.

We often make new words by adding suffixes. For example, we got the word *syndication* by adding the *-ion* suffix to the end of the verb *syndicate*. But the process can also work in reverse: we can make new words by dropping suffixes. For example, we got the verb *edit* by dropping the suffix from *editor*. That's called back formation, and it's how lexicographers think we got the word *orientate*—by dropping the *-ion* suffix from *orientation*.

Orient and *orientate* are both acceptable English verbs, but *orient* is preferred in American English and *orientate* is preferred in British English.

What Should You Do?

In American English, stick with *orient*.

> **The way you move—you** orient **yourself around him without even thinking about it. When he moves, even a little bit, you adjust your position at the same time. Like magnets . . . or gravity. You're like a . . . satellite, or something.**
>
> —Stephenie Meyer in *Eclipse*

Over

✦ What's the Trouble? Many people have been taught not to use **over** to mean *more than,* but there is no basis for the rule.

More than and *over* both have multiple meanings, but when the words act as a preposition before a number, they're usually equivalent: *More than twenty camels performed a ballet. Over twenty camels performed a ballet.*

The "rule" against using *over* in this sense originated with an influential *New York Evening Post* editor in 1877. Despite having no rationale, his dictum propagated throughout newspaper style guides becoming what *Merriam-Webster's Dictionary of English Usage* calls a "hoary American newspaper tradition."

Nearly all modern style guides come out strongly against the "rule." *Garner's Modern American Usage* calls it a "baseless crotchet" and *The American Heritage Guide to Contemporary Usage and Style* says it may be "safely ignored." Even the newest edition of the *AP Stylebook* (a hoary American newspaper style book!) takes a softened stance on *over,* saying that *more than* is "preferred with numerals," but not going so far as to say that *over* is wrong.

What Should You Do?

Unless you work for a publication that follows AP style, freely use *over* to mean *more than* if it works better in your sentence.

> **Miracle of love. You're** over **twice as likely to be killed by the person you love than by a stranger.**
>
> —Hugh Laurie as Dr. Gregory House in the TV series *House M.D.*

Now, you listen to me, officer. I do not take kindly to you shining your light in the eyes of my female companion. And as I have more than 100 years on you, I do not take kindly to you calling me "son."

—Stephen Moyer as Bill Compton in the
TV series *True Blood*

Pair

✦ **What's the Trouble?** People find **pair** confusing. Is it singular or plural? When should you use *pairs*?

A *pair* is "two of something," but *a pair of* can be singular or plural—it's one of those odd English verbs (like *couple*) that can be singular or plural depending on how you're thinking of the people or items in question.

> **A** pair **of papers . . . have been submitted to Astronomy and Astrophysics, describing the planets.**
>
> —Dennis Overbye writing for *The New York Times*

> **In the crowd, furious but friendly arguments were taking place as surrounding groups watched, much the way one-on-one basketball games are enjoyed in urban America. One** pair **was arguing the merits of salvaging at least a bit of the Russian language as Ukrainians try to move forward into independence.**
>
> —Francis X. Clines writing for *The New York Times*

Sometimes you'll see *pair* (without an s at the end) used as a plural noun, but *pairs* is the better choice in such instances.

What Should You Do?

When you're talking about more than one pair, the plural is *pairs*: *I own one pair of pants. I own eight pairs of pants.*

A pair of can take a singular or plural verb, depending on your meaning. Choose the verb that best reflects the singleness or plurality of your sentence.

Percent

✦ **What's the Trouble?** Writers who aren't comfortable with math can confuse **percent** with *percentage points*.

When you are writing about increases or decreases in measurements that are themselves percents, it's often important to be painfully clear whether your changes are *percent changes* or *percentage point changes*.

For example, if 6 percent of students attended swim meets last year, and 8 percent of students attended swim meets this year, that's a 33 *percent* increase in attendance, but an increase of only 2 *percentage points*.

See how the way you present the number can influence how dramatic the change seems? Also, if you use the wrong word, you can be very far from reality.

What Should You Do?

Use care when writing about *percent changes*.

> **DARNELL JACKSON: Uh, what** percentage **in chance does my friend, Aki, have of sleeping with you?**
>
> **YUN: Zero** percent.
>
> **DARNELL JACKSON: One more question, please. What if he's a professional break-dancer?**
>
> **YUN: Two** percent.
>
> **AKI: Mathematically that's an infinity** percent **increase.**
>
> —Miguel A. Núñez Jr. as Darnell, Kira Clavell as Yun, and Bobby Lee as Aki in the movie *Kickin' It Old Skool*

Peruse

✦ **What's the Trouble?** **Peruse** is misunderstood in more than one way.

Peruse means "read," and it has for centuries, but in 1906 an influential editor named Frank Vizetelly pronounced, without any reasoning, that *peruse* should only mean "to read with care and attention." His pronouncement was included in multiple books under his sway, and those books influenced later usage guides.

Although *peruse* is occasionally used metaphorically, it doesn't mean "browse"; you don't peruse clothes in a store, for example.

What Should You Do?

You may certainly use *peruse* to mean "read carefully," but do not cringe when you see it used to simply mean "read." Using *peruse* to mean "skim" isn't advisable, and using it to mean "browse" is clearly wrong.

> **Bessie asked if I would have a book: the word book acted as a transient stimulus, and I begged her to fetch *Gulliver's Travels* from the library. This book I had again and again perused with delight.**
>
> —Charlotte Brontë in *Jane Eyre*

Plethora

✦ **What's the Trouble?** Usage guides disagree about how acceptable it is to use **plethora** to mean simply "many."

Traditionally, *plethora* has meant "an unpleasant overabundance of something," but people often use it to mean simply "a lot of a bad thing" (instead of "too much of a bad thing") or even "a lot of a good thing." Some usage writers still find this change outrageous, and others consider it almost fully acceptable.

What Should You Do?

Using *plethora* to describe a happy bounty isn't the worst mistake you could make—usage is clearly going in that direction—but for the time being, use *plethora* only when your cup is metaphorically overflowing with something unpleasant.

> **The number of games is obscene . . . The initial repercussion of this** plethora **of games was to commoditize them all, but with so many games, special places like Notre Dame become more important.**
>
> —Ken Schanzer, president of NBC Universal Sports, in an interview with *The New York Times*

Preventative

✦ What's the Trouble? English has two words that mean the same thing: *preventive* and **preventative.**

Often when we have two nearly identical words that mean the same thing, such as *preventive* and *preventative*, everyone presumes that one of them is wrong—usually the longer one. Such logic would suggest that *preventative* is a bad word.

You will certainly find occasional admonitions against *preventative*, but most sources consider it to be Standard English. It's been around as an adjective and a noun for over three hundred years.

What Should You Do?

You may certainly choose to use the sleeker *preventive*, but don't chide people who prefer the longer form.

> Preventive **war is like committing suicide out of fear of death.**
>
> —Otto von Bismarck, first chancellor of the German Empire

> **The primary focus for** preventative **care in ferrets should be centered on yearly or biyearly physical examination.**
>
> —Bonnie M. Ballard and Ryan Cheek in *Exotic Animal Medicine for the Veterinary Technician*

Rack

✦ What's the Trouble? *Wrack* is starting to encroach on **rack**, but the two words aren't interchangeable.

We have racks for storing spices and drying clothes, but in the Middle Ages, the rack was an instrument for torture. The "mental torment" meaning of *rack* in *rack your brain* and *nerve-racking* comes from the idea of physical torment of bodies on the rack.

On the other hand, the word *wrack* is related to the word *wreck*, meaning "damage or destruction." Since *rack* and *wrack* sound similar and have similar meanings, people can get them confused, but *rack your brain* and *nerve-racking* are set phrases, as is *wrack and ruin*.

What Should You Do?

Remember that the set phrases are *rack your brain* and *nerve-racking*.

QUICK AND DIRTY TIP

When you <u>rack</u> your brain or make it through a nerve-<u>racking</u> exam, think of yourself as being tortured on the <u>rack</u> in the Middle Ages.

I think about death all the time, but only in a romantic, self-serving way, beginning, most often, with my tragic illness and ending with my funeral. I see my brother squatting beside my grave, so racked by guilt that he's unable to stand. "If only I'd paid him back that twenty-five thousand dollars I borrowed," he says. I see Hugh, drying his eyes on the sleeve of his suit jacket, then crying even harder when he remembers I bought it for him.

—David Sedaris in *When You Are Engulfed in Flames*

Real

✦ What's the Trouble? Real shouldn't be used as an adverb, but it is.

The basic rules are simple: *really* is an adverb (*I really like cheese*), and *real* is an adjective (*Nothing beats real Parmesan cheese*).

In practice, however, in informal conversation and among people who use folksy language (either naturally or in a calculating way, as politicians sometimes do), *real* is also often used as an intensifying adverb that means "very."

What Should You Do?

Unless you're going for a colloquial sound, as in the following two examples, avoid using *real* as an adverb.

> **Why shouldn't I work for the N.S.A.? That's a tough one, but I'll take a shot. Say I'm working at N.S.A. Somebody puts a code on my desk, something nobody else can break.**

Maybe I take a shot at it and maybe I break it. And I'm real happy with myself, 'cause I did my job well. But maybe that code was the location of some rebel army in North Africa or the Middle East. Once they have that location, they bomb the village where the rebels were hiding and fifteen hundred people I never met, never had no problem with, get killed.

—Matt Damon as Will in the movie *Good Will Hunting*

That's one of those issues that if you don't say exactly the right word, exactly the way somebody expects it, you step on a landmine. That's why we wrote it down. So we could be real clear.

—Herman Cain, American politician

Shine

✦ **What's the Trouble?** The verb **shine** has two past tense forms: *shined* and *shone*.

Shined and *shone* are two competing, acceptable past tense forms of the verb *shine*. Some (but not all) sources recommend using *shined* when the verb has an object (when you are shining something) and *shone* when it does not (when something is shining on its own).

Meaning matters though too: *shined* is the only acceptable past tense when you mean "polished," as in *He shined his shoes*.

What Should You Do?

Stick with the traditional rule of using *shined* with an object and *shone* without unless you have a good reason to deviate.

QUICK AND DIRTY TIP

The rhyme *it's shone when alone* will help you remember to use *shone* when the verb is alone (i.e., has no object).

Mr. Robinson was a polished sort of person. He was so clean and healthy and pleased about everything that he positively shone— **which is only to be expected in a fairy or an angel, but is somewhat disconcerting in an attorney.**

—Susanna Clarke, *Jonathan Strange & Mr. Norrell*

If you want the law to leave you alone, keep your hair trimmed and your boots shined.

—Louis L'Amour in *The Man Called Noon*

Since

✦ **What's the Trouble?** **Since** can be used to mean "because," but sometimes doing so creates ambiguity.

Since can carry an element of time, but *since* and *because* have also been synonyms throughout the ages. *Since we still had money in our pockets, we decided to try blackjack* means the same thing as *Because we still had money in our pockets, we decided to try blackjack*.

Sometimes, however, a sentence with *since* can be interpreted two ways, and that is when you should avoid using *since* to mean *because*. Consider this ambiguous sentence from Hunter S. Thompson: *Life has become immeasurably better since I have been forced to stop taking it seriously*. He probably means "life is better since the time he was forced to stop taking it seriously," but he could also mean "life is better because he was forced to stop taking it seriously."

What Should You Do?

Don't be afraid to use *since* as a synonym for *because*. Just be sure you aren't creating ambiguous sentences.

Laughter and tears are both responses to frustration and exhaustion. . . . I myself prefer to laugh, since **there is less cleaning do to do afterward.**

—Kurt Vonnegut in *Palm Sunday*

Since

Fear isn't so difficult to understand. After all, weren't we all frightened as children? Nothing has changed since **Little Red Riding Hood** faced the big bad wolf. What frightens us today is exactly the same sort of thing that frightened us yesterday. It's just a different wolf.

—Alfred Hitchcock quoted in *It's Only a Movie*
by Charlotte Chandler

Slow

✦ What's the Trouble? Misguided sticklers often insist that **slow** can never be an adverb.

English has a class of words called flat adverbs: the adjective can be used as an adverb (such as *slow, quick,* and *loud*) even when a separate adverb that ends in *-ly* exists (such as *slowly, quickly,* and *loudly*). Although you can use the *-ly* adverb form if you prefer (*drive slowly*), it is also acceptable to use the flat adverb (*drive slow*).

Despite vocal sticklers who rail against *drive slow* (including Weird Al Yankovic, who made a funny video about it), every major style guide and dictionary say it and other instances of flat adverbs are fine. Even William Strunk, of *Elements of Style* fame, was known to say, "If you don't know how to pronounce a word, say it loud!" Additional examples of flat adverbs appear regularly in poems and literature.

What Should You Do?

You may want to avoid flat adverbs in situations in which it could be a problem if you're perceived to have made a mistake (such as in a résumé cover letter), but in general writing, if a flat adverb fits better in your sentence, don't be afraid to use it.

Talk low, talk slow, and don't say too much.

—John Wayne quoted in *The Elephant to Hollywood*
by Michael Caine

Smokey

✦ What's the Trouble? The word has two spellings.

Between Smokey Robinson, Smokey the Bear, and the movie *Smokey and the Bandit,* you can be forgiven for thinking the correct spelling for the smell of burned wood is **smokey,** but you're still wrong. The correct spelling is *smoky.* When it's a nickname for an officer of the law, it's spelled *smokey,* but otherwise, drop the *e.*

What Should You Do?

Use this Quick and Dirty Tip to remember that a policeman's or ranger's nickname is *Smokey,* with an *e*: Think of officers as keeping their eyes on *you*—*eyes,* with all those *e*'s.

> **TINA:** [concerned about a sniper outside] **But what happens if he hits the gas tank?**
>
> **MATT HELM:** Smokey **the Bear won't like it. Get in.**
>
> —Daliah Lavi as Tina and Dean Martin as Matt Helm in the movie *The Silencers*

> **[cooking a mushroom over the chimney] The key is to keep turning it to get the** smoky **flavor nice and even.**
>
> —Patton Oswalt voicing Remy in the movie *Ratatouille*

South

✦ What's the Trouble? Sometimes directional terms such as **south** are capitalized and sometimes they aren't.

When you're describing a direction, *south* is lowercase: *The map is behind a secret door on the south wall*.

When you're naming a region, however, *South* is capitalized. Atlanta, New Orleans, and Mobile are all in the *South,* not the *south.* The same holds true for other directional terms that are also the names of regions: Midwest, Northeast, Northwest, Middle East, and so on. Often, if you can put *the* in front of the name, it's capitalized: *He's from the South.*

When directional terms are used to describe people, style guides offer differing advice. For example, *The Chicago Manual of Style* prefers *southerner,* whereas the Associated Press prefers *Southerner.*

South

What Should You Do?

If a directional term is the name of a region, capitalize it. If it's just a compass point, lowercase it.

> **This is Berk. It's twelve days north of Hopeless and a few degrees south of Freezing to Death. It's located solidly on the Meridian of Misery.**
>
> —Jay Baruchel voicing Hiccup in the movie
> *How to Train Your Dragon*

> **Here's a soldier of the South who loves you, Scarlett. Wants to feel your arms around him, wants to carry the memory of your kisses into battle with him. Never mind about loving me, you're a woman sending a soldier to his death with a beautiful memory. Scarlett! Kiss me! Kiss me . . . once. . . .**
>
> —Clark Gable as Rhett Butler in the movie
> *Gone with the Wind*

Team

✦ **What's the Trouble?** People wonder whether collective nouns such as **team** are singular or plural.

Teams, committees, boards, and bands are made up of lots of people, but the words are collective nouns and in the United States, we generally treat them as singular. (In Britain, writers are more likely to treat them as plural.)

Names of teams (and bands) are different however. The rules are less clear, and most writers treat the names differently depending on whether they sound singular or plural. For example, we'd write that the *Beatles are* one of the bestselling bands of all time, but that *Radiohead is* on tour.

What Should You Do?

In the United States, treat collective nouns such as *team* as singular and team names as singular unless the name itself sounds plural.

> **Your team is dealing with the Great Mayonnaise Panic of 2007. I'm worried it might spread to other continents.**
>
> —Lisa Edelstein as Dr. Lisa Cuddy in the TV series *House M.D.*

> **JAMES STAMPHILL: How do you think the Yankees will do against the Redskins this year?**
>
> **HENRI YOUNG: The Yankees are a baseball team. The Redskins are a football team. Personally, I think the Redskins would kick the **** out of them.**
>
> —Christian Slater as James Stamphill and Kevin Bacon as Henri Young in the movie *Murder in the First*

Than I Versus Than Me

✦ **What's the Trouble?** People argue about which pronoun to use in sentences such as *Nobody loves grammar more* **than** *[I/me]*.

The trouble with sentences that end with *than me* is that sometimes they can be ambiguous. *You like Quinn more than me* could mean that "you like Quinn more than you like me," or that "you like Quinn more than I like Quinn."

> **FINN HUDSON: Okay, Rachel, since this is your first time at this, I'm gonna break it down for you. Guys and girls fall into certain archetypes when they get drunk. Exhibit A: Santana, the weepy, hysterical drunk.**
>
> **SANTANA LOPEZ: [Weeping at Sam] You like her** more than me. **She's blonde and awesome and so smart. Admit, just admit it! No, kiss me!**
>
> —Cory Monteith as Finn and Naya Rivera as
> Santana in the TV series *Glee*

What Should You Do?

When ending a sentence with *than me* would create ambiguity, but *I* alone would sound too stuffy, add the implied word that follows: *You like Quinn more than I* do.

Also keep in mind that even when there is no ambiguity, *than I* has a more formal tone than *than me,* and you should keep your audience in mind when choosing your pronoun. *Quinn is smarter than I* sounds more buttoned up than *Quinn is smarter than me.*

> **BLAIR WALDORF: What are you doing here? Making sure the Dean knows it's all my fault?**
>
> **SERENA VAN DER WOODSEN: No. I came to tell him that Yale is your dream and you deserve to go here** more than I do. **What are you doing here?**
>
> **BLAIR WALDORF: Doing the same thing for you.**
>
> —Leighton Meester as Blair and Blake Lively as Serena in the TV series *Gossip Girl*

They

✦ What's the Trouble? English doesn't have a singular pronoun to use when you don't know the person's sex.

English has a big, gaping hole: no pronoun we can use to describe a person when we don't know their sex (see!)—I've tried *it* with babies, and it hasn't gone well. In days gone by, *he* was acceptable as a generic pronoun, but today it's not. Nearly all major style guides recommend against it.

To fill the gap, many people consciously or subconsciously use **they**, as in *Tell the next caller they win a car.* Doing so actually has a longer history than most people realize and is allowed by some current style guides. Although many people consider it wrong, I suspect many of those same people say it in casual conversation without even realizing it and that the singular *they* will become fully acceptable within the next fifty years.

Sentences that start with singular pronouns that sound plural (such as *everyone*) cause particular temptation to use *they* or *their* as singular pronouns later in the sentence.

What Should You Do?

If being perceived as making a mistake could be a problem (e.g., in résumé cover letters), rewrite your sentences to avoid using *they* as a singular pronoun. Making the subject plural is often an easy solution.

> **Everybody around her was gay and busy; each had** their **object of interest,** their **part,** their **dress,** their **favourite scene,** their **friends and confederates: all were finding employment in consultations and comparisons, or**

diversion in the playful conceits they sug-
gested. [*Each* is always singular, yet Austen used
their.]

—Jane Austen in *Mansfield Park*

**Everybody is always supposing that I'm not a
good walker; and yet** they **would not have
been pleased if we had refused to join them.**
[*Everybody* is always singular, yet Austen used
they.]

—Jane Austen in *Persuasion*

Toward

✦ What's the Trouble? Sometimes you'll see **toward**, and sometimes you'll see *towards*.

Toward is the typical spelling in the United States in all cases, but the British will often use *toward* as an adjective and *towards* as an adverb. This sometimes causes confusion for American readers of British publications.

The rule holds for all *-ward* suffixes. The preferred American forms are *afterward, outward, forward, backward,* and so on.

What Should You Do?

Use this Quick and Dirty Tip: Remember that the American spelling is *toward* by thinking that Americans like shortcuts, so we've lopped off the *s*.

> **May I have everyone's attention, please?
> We're evacuating into outer space, with
> literally infinite directions in which to flee.
> However, we have decided that our transports
> will travel directly** toward **the fleet of Star
> Destroyers. Any questions?**
>
> —Alex Borstein voicing Lois Griffin as Princess Leia
> in the TV series *Family Guy*

Try And

✦ What's the Trouble? Try and is considered less acceptable than *try to*.

Although *try and* has been used in speech and informal writing for centuries, it has also often been condemned. Usage guides of old recommended against it, and radio callers today still regularly cite it as a pet peeve. Nevertheless, modern experts call *try and* informal, not wrong.

It appears that in the mid-1800s *try and* and *try to* were used about equally, but since then *try to* has become the dominant form in print. *Try and* may be slightly more common in print in Britain than in America, but *try to* is the more common form in both regions.

What Should You Do?

Avoid *try and* in formal writing but don't go ballistic if somebody says it in conversation or writes it in an e-mail.

> **I recognize terror as the finest emotion and so I will** try to **terrorize the reader. But if I find that I cannot terrify, I will** try to **horrify, and if I find that I cannot horrify, I'll go for the gross-out. I'm not proud.**
>
> —Stephen King in *Stephen King's Danse Macabre*

> **If you** try and **take a cat apart to see how it works, the first thing you have on your hands is a non-working cat.**
>
> —Douglas Adams quoted in *A Devil's Chaplain: Reflections on Hope, Lies, Science, and Love* by Richard Dawkins

Twins

✦ **What's the Trouble?** Some people insist that a pair of **twins** is four people.

Some overly literal people argue that since *twins* already means "two people," a pair of twins is four people. However, *a pair of twins* is the common idiom to refer to "two people who happen to be twins."

What Should You Do?

A pair of twins is "two people"; don't be afraid to use the phrase. However, notice your context and be sure it won't cause confusion. Ask yourself if *twins* alone or *two* in place of *twins* would be just as good.

> **In the backseat Moose and Squirrel inhabited a pair of six-year-old-twins, and wouldn't stop bickering and picking their noses. They were clearly in their element.**
>
> —Neal Shusterman in *Everwild*

Unique

✦ What's the Trouble? **Unique** is an absolute term, but it's common to hear people modify it, saying such things as *very unique*.

Grammarians call adjectives such as *unique, dead,* and *impossible* "ungradable." It means they can't be more of what they already are. If something is already impossible, it can't get *more* impossible. *Unique* means "one of a kind" or "having no equal," and things can't become more unique. Thus, although you often see descriptions that include *very unique* on Craigslist, real estate sites, and in personal ads, the phrasing is wrong.

Gradable terms can be modified down, however. For example, *almost unique* is fine, just as it would be fine to describe something as *almost impossible* or *almost dead*.

What Should You Do?

Reserve *unique* for things that are truly one of a kind.

> **HENRY VAN STATTEN: Tell them to stop shooting at it!**
>
> **DIANA GODDARD: But it's killing them.**
>
> **HENRY VAN STATTEN: They're dispensable. That Dalek's unique. I don't want a scratch on its bodywork. Do you hear me? Do you hear me?**
>
> —Corey Johnson as Henry Van Statten and
> Anna-Louise Plowman as Diana Goddard
> in the TV series *Doctor Who*

Until

+ **What's the Trouble?** When used to describe a deadline, **until** can be ambiguous.

If you have *until* March 4 to submit an entry in the National Grammar Day video contest, does that mean you can still turn it in on March 4, or is March 3 the last acceptable day? Unfortunately, the word *until* doesn't make the meaning clear.

One of the most stress-inducing deadlines is the annual tax filing deadline for the Internal Revenue Service, which makes a point to spell out that the April 15 filing deadline includes April 15. They also call April 15 a due date, not a deadline.

What Should You Do?

If you're following instructions, don't assume *until* means *through*. Turn in your item a day early or get clarification. If you're writing instructions, make them clear by using a word such as *through* or stating a specific day and time. The IRS doesn't rely on an ambiguous word such as *until,* and neither should you.

> **The end of the world started when a pegasus landed on the hood of my car. Up** until **then I was having a great afternoon.** [*Until* ends with the landing.]
>
> —Rick Riordan in *The Last Olympian*

> **"But I have to confess, I'm glad you two had at least a few months of happiness together."**
> **"I'm not glad," says Peeta. "I wish we had waited** until **the whole thing was done officially."** [*Until* seems to go through the time it is done.]
>
> —Suzanne Collins in *Catching Fire*

Utilize

✦ **What's the Trouble?** Writers sometimes choose **utilize** when *use* would suffice.

Often, you can replace *utilize* with *use* and your sentence will mean the same thing and sound less stuffy.

Utilize does have its uses, though. It conveys more of a sense of using something specifically for a purpose or for profit than *use* does. You may use a camera, but it may be more descriptive to say that propagandists utilize cameras to influence opinions, since that is their purpose and it's more specialized than just snapping photos.

What Should You Do?

Don't use *utilize* just because it sounds like a fancy word. When in doubt, choose *use*. On the other hand, don't be afraid to use *utilize* when you're confident that it's the right word.

> **Because we humans are big and clever enough to produce and** utilize **antibiotics and disinfectants, it is easy to convince ourselves that we have banished bacteria to the fringes of existence. Don't you believe it. Bacteria may not build cities or have interesting social lives, but they will be here when the Sun explodes. This is their planet, and we are on it only because they allow us to be.**
>
> —Bill Bryson in *A Short History of Nearly Everything*

Verbal

✦ **What's the Trouble?** **Verbal** can mean "written" as well as "spoken."

You may be surprised to learn that *verbal* can mean "written" as well as "spoken," and even more surprised that some people believe you should never use *verbal* to mean "spoken" and should instead use *oral* in such circumstances.

Although using *verbal* to mean "written" is legitimate, history and common usage are not on the side of people who would like to say *verbal* can't also mean "spoken." In fact, it is relatively easy to find quotations in which *verbal* is used to mean "spoken" in direct contrast with *written*. Also, the "spoken" meaning is so common that it's likely some readers will be confused if you use *verbal* to mean "written."

What Should You Do?

Use *verbal* to mean "written" if you wish, but be sure your context makes the meaning clear. Do not hesitate to use *verbal* to mean "spoken."

> **The real history of Africa is still in the custody of black storytellers and wise men, black historians, medicine men: it is a** verbal **history, still kept safe from the white man and his predations. Everywhere, if you keep your mind open, you will find the words** *not* **written down.**
>
> —Nobel Laureate Doris Lessing in *The Golden Notebook*

Website

✦ **What's the Trouble?** People commonly write both **website** and *Web site*.

Open compounds often become closed compounds over time, so although *Web site* was more common when the Internet was new and we were just starting to describe the sites that appear on the Web, the closed compound, *website,* is now the most commonly recommended spelling.

You may be wondering why *Web site* is capitalized but *website* is not. It isn't related to the newness or importance of the Web, it's because of the regular English capitalization rules: we capitalized words that are the name of something specific, and most sources agree that the Web, which is short for the World Wide Web, is an entity made up of all the files that are accessible on the Internet by using the HTTP protocol. There is only one, and its name is the Web—a proper noun. On the other hand there are millions (gazillions?) of sites on the Web, so *website* is merely descriptive—a common noun.

The capitalization of *Web* is a subject of debate, however. *The Chicago Manual of Style* used to recommend *Web,* but recently switched to *web* in the new 16th edition, stating that they now consider *web* a generic term. So far, they are an outlier, but that could change in the future.

What Should You Do?

Most major style guides recommend *website,* so write it that way unless you work for an editor who requires otherwise.

The website **didn't say how much brains—or even how many—I should eat, only that I**

should eat them in 48 hours OR ELSE. Why doesn't anyone pay attention to details anymore? Would it be so hard to add a simple line like, BTW, Maddy, 3 pounds of brains per week is plenty?

Seriously, am I the first new zombie ever to ask?

—Rusty Fischer in *Zombies Don't Cry*

While looking at a website for liposuction, I learned that it was a six-to-eight-week recovery period, the clincher being that, during that time, I would under no circumstances be able to use street drugs. Obviously I had to think of a more realistic approach.

—Chelsea Handler in *Are You There, Vodka? It's Me, Chelsea*

Whet

✦ **What's the Trouble?** People confuse **whet** and *wet*.

Whet means "to sharpen or incite." You *whet a blade,* but you also *whet your appetite*. However, people sometimes write *wet your appetite* instead. People may think of salivating when they think of an increasing appetite or confuse the phrase with *wet your whistle,* which means "to take a drink" (and which, to add to the confusion, the *Oxford English Dictionary* says is also sometimes written as *whet your whistle).*

What Should You Do?

Remember that the correct phrases are *whet your appetite* and *wet your whistle.*

QUICK AND DIRTY TIP

Think of a <u>whetted</u> knife cutting scrumptious meat when you think of <u>whetting</u> your appetite. Unless you're a vegetarian. Then imagine the knife cutting scrumptious squash.

No doubt the murderous knife was dull before it was whetted **on your stone-hard heart.**

—Annette Bening as Queen Elizabeth in
the movie *Richard III*

While

✦ What's the Trouble? Some people believe **while** should not mean "although."

Some meanings of *while* have a sense of time, such as "during," "at the same time as," or "a length of time." *While* has another meaning, however, which has sometimes raised hackles: *while* can be used as a synonym for *although* or *whereas*.

Although *while* is perfectly acceptable to use in this way, occasionally doing so can cause ambiguity. For example, if you were to say, *While Squiggly is yellow, Aardvark is blue,* people wouldn't know whether you were contrasting the two characters' colors or saying that Aardvark is only blue *when* Squiggly is yellow. In cases like that, you have to use *although* or *whereas*.

What Should You Do?

You can choose to limit the meaning of *while* to senses of time in your own writing if you like, but don't correct others who choose to use the wider meaning.

> **Any man who can drive safely** while **kissing a pretty girl is simply not giving the kiss the attention it deserves.**
>
> —Albert Einstein

> **Just so you know,** while **there are few things I consider sacred, the back of the limo is one of them.**
>
> —Ed Westwick as Chuck Bass in the TV series *Gossip Girl*

Whom

✦ **What's the Trouble?** Writers have long been predicting the demise of **whom**. Few people know how to use it properly in every instance, and yet it persists.

Many language lovers cringe at the suggestion that we should just get rid of *whom,* but the suggestions and the predictions that it will happen have been around since at least the late 1800s, and *who* is often used in place of *whom,* even by the well educated and well heeled, especially in speech.

In a 2008 *Visual Thesaurus* set of articles, even John McIntyre, who was then the assistant managing editor of the copy desk at *The Baltimore Sun* and the former president of the American Copy Editors Society and had been chosen to champion the cause of *whom,* could only muster a tepid defense: "For now, *whom,* though it may have seen its best days, is going, going, but not quite gone."

Since *whom*'s demise has been predicted for at least 150 years and yet it still continues to cling to life (albeit precariously), it's still worth knowing the rules and attempting to follow them. It's not likely that style guides will just give up on *whom* in the near future, and a good number of people will still write angry e-mails or mark your papers with red ink if you get it wrong.

What Should You Do?

In writing and unless doing so sounds painfully stilted, follow the standard rule: Use *who* for the subject of a sentence and *whom* for the object of a sentence or the object of a preposition (e.g., when it follows words such as *for, of,* and *with*).

Whom

NANCY: [after seeing that the house is now fully secured] **Mother! What's with the bars?**

MARGE: **Security.**

NANCY: **Security? Security from what?**

MARGE: **Not from what, from whom.**

—Heather Langenkamp as Nancy and Ronee Blakley as Marge in the movie *A Nightmare on Elm Street*

Wool

✦ What's the Trouble? Because the noun **wool** has the related adjective *woolen*, some people believe it is incorrect to describe something as a *wool sweater* or *wool jacket*.

Nouns regularly serve as adjectives in English. When they do, we call them attributive nouns. For example, <u>California</u> style includes many things: <u>tree</u> farms, <u>cotton</u> clothing, and <u>avocado</u> sandwiches. All the underlined words are attributive nouns.

Not all nouns have related adjectives. *Cotton* and *fleece,* for example, are your only choice for describing a cotton shirt or fleece jacket. Since *wool* and *silk* have the adjective forms *woolen* and *silken,* you get to choose between the attributive noun and adjective. You can wear a silken scarf with your woolen sweater, or you can wear a silk scarf with your wool sweater, for example. Until the 1970s *wool* and *woolen* appeared about equally, but *wool* is now used far more often than *woolen*.

What Should You Do?

Feel free to use nouns such as *wool* and *silk* as adjectives.

> **Feds aren't like that. Feds are serious people. Poli-sci majors. Student council presidents. Debate club chairpersons. The kinds of people who have the grit to wear a dark** wool **suit and a tightly buttoned collar even when the temperature has greenhoused up to a hundred and ten degrees and the humidity is thick enough to stall a jumbo jet. The kinds of people who feel most at home on the dark side of a one-way mirror.**
>
> —Neal Stephenson in *Snow Crash*

Wrong

+ What's the Trouble? Some people think **wrong** can't be used as an adverb.

Wrongly only acts as an adverb, and the word comes up a lot in news stories: people are *wrongly arrested, wrongly jailed, wrongly convicted,* and *wrongly released.*

Although some people believe that since we already have the adverb *wrongly,* it must be the only choice. Wrong! *Wrong,* can also be an adverb—and a noun, verb, and adjective too. (Who knew there were so many ways to go wrong?)

Most often, *wrong* sounds right when it comes after a verb, as in *gone wrong, heard wrong,* and *you're doing it wrong;* and *wrongly* sounds right when it comes before the verb, as in *wrongly accused.*

What Should You Do?

Don't be afraid to use *wrong* as an adverb. Trust your ear.

> **Dewey Bozella—who was** wrongly **jailed for 26 years—won his first professional boxing match since being let out of prison for a murder he didn't commit.**
>
> —Emily Hewett in *Metro*

> **Sometimes I lie awake at night, and I ask, "Where have I gone** wrong."
>
> **Then a voice says to me, "This is going to take more than one night."**
>
> —Charlie Brown in the Charles M. Schulz comic strip *Peanuts*

You and I

+ **What's the Trouble?** Between **you and I** is so widespread in popular culture that people are becoming confused.

Pronouns that follow prepositions (such as *between, of,* and *about*) in prepositional phrases are always in the objective case. That means that the correct phrase is always *between you and me,* but people seem to have a hard time remembering that rule.

Unfortunately, popular songs have gotten it wrong and increased the confusion. For example, Jessica Simpson released a song with the title "Between You and I" (which should have been "You and Me" because it follows the preposition *between*). The 2010 Olympic theme song included "I believe in the power of *you and I*" (which should have been *you and me* because it follows the preposition *of*), and Bryan Adams wrote "That would change if she ever found out about *you and I*" (which should have been *you and me* because it follows the preposition *about*).

You and I

Actually, the pronoun confusion isn't even limited to prepositional phrases; they're just common offenders. For example,
Lady Gaga wrote "*You and me* could write a bad romance"
(which should have been "*You and I* could write a bad romance" because the pronouns are in the subject position).

What Should You Do?

Remember to use object prepositions (e.g., *me, him*) after prepositions and that the correct phrase is *between you and me*.

> **PENNY: This is** between you and me. **You can't
> tell Leonard any of this.**
>
> **SHELDON COOPER: You're asking me to keep a
> secret?**
>
> **PENNY: Yeah.**
>
> **SHELDON COOPER: Well, I am sorry, but you
> would have had to have expressed that desire
> before revealing the secret, so that I could
> choose whether I wanted to accept the
> covenant of secret-keeping. You can't impose
> a secret on an ex-post-facto basis.**
>
> —Kaley Cuoco as Penny and Jim Parsons as Sheldon
> in the TV series *The Big Bang Theory*

Acknowledgments

Thank you to Mario Sanchez from New Mexico, who found the "next Wednesday" quotation; Joe Kisenwether from Reno, Nevada, who explained odds to me; my editor, Beata Santora; my agent, Laurie Abkemeier; my Facebook and Twitter friends; and the Grammar Girl podcast listeners.

I used the following sources extensively: *Garner's Modern American Usage, Merriam-Webster's Dictionary of English Usage, The Columbia Guide to Standard American English, The American Heritage Guide to Contemporary Usage and Style, The Chicago Manual of Style, AP Stylebook,* the online *Oxford English Dictionary,* M-W.com, and Dictionary.com. I also occasionally consulted *Fowler's Modern English Usage, The Yahoo! Style Guide,* and various other sources. I primarily found quotations through GoodReads.com, IMDb.com, Google News, and Google Books, although I occasionally searched other sources.

About the Author

Mignon Fogarty is the creator of Quick and Dirty Tips. Formerly a magazine writer, technical writer, and entrepreneur, she has a B.A. in English from the University of Washington in Seattle and an M.S. in biology from Stanford University. She lives in Reno, Nevada. Visit her website at quickanddirtytips.com and sign up for the free e-mail grammar tips and free podcast.

Quick and Dirty Tips™

Helping you do things better.